THE
DOCTOR'S
WIDOW

BOOKS BY DANIEL HURST

The Doctor's Wife

The Holiday Home

Til Death Do Us Part

The Passenger

The Woman at the Door

He Was a Liar

The Wrong Woman

We Used to Live Here

The Couple at Table Six

We Tell No One

The Accident

What My Family Saw

The Intruder

The Couple in the Cabin

THE
DOCTOR'S
WIDOW

DANIEL HURST

Bookouture

Published by Bookouture in 2023

An imprint of Storyfire Ltd.
Carmelite House
50 Victoria Embankment
London EC4Y 0DZ

www.bookouture.com

ISBN: 978-1-83790-826-4
eBook ISBN: 978-1-83790-825-7

PROLOGUE

The police really thought they had me when they kicked down my door and burst into my home.

They burst through the new door that belonged to the expensive house that I'd only just bought. When I settled the estate agent's fees and accepted the keys, I had no idea the beautiful property I had purchased would soon be swarming with police officers.

But it was.

Dozens of men and women, all of them in black and white uniforms, and all of them eager to wrap my wrists in handcuffs and march me outside to one of the waiting vehicles, while my new neighbours stopped and stared at the unsavoury scene happening right in front of them on their quiet street in an affluent suburb.

That was their plan anyway. But, as has been the case for a while now, the police's plan has always differed greatly from my own.

As the boots belonging to several officers trod over my plush new carpet, I was elsewhere, miles away, in a different part of the country, which was fortunate for me and unfortunate for them. As they pushed open freshly glossed doors and inspected freshly painted rooms, I was nowhere to be seen, which meant their superiors were not going to be happy when the news filtered back to them that no arrest was made. As the entire property, one that had cost me almost a million pounds when I'd bought it two weeks earlier, was ransacked for any hint or clue that might tell the police where the owner was now located, I was already planning to do the one thing they were there to make me do.

I was planning to go to prison.

But just like everything else in my life, I was going to do it on my terms and no one else's.

As the search of my home was completed and the police officers returned to their cars emptyhanded, my neighbours would have slowly gone back inside their own houses, some perhaps relieved that there had been no arrests made so close to their home, but a few were presumably a little disappointed not to witness even more of a spectacular show right on their doorsteps.

Was I sorry to disappoint them? Did I wish I could have been there to really give them something to gossip about?

Did you see the police come to arrest our new neighbour – Fern?

What do you think she did?

I heard she killed her husband and almost got away with it. Do you think it's true?

I heard she killed more than one person.

Really? She didn't seem like a killer to me.

I don't know, you can never judge a book by its cover.

That was most likely just some of the conversations that went on behind closed doors on my street not long after all but two of the police officers had left and returned to the station. The pair who stayed behind had a simple task. They were to sit inside their vehicle and keep watch on my house on the off-chance that I returned. If so, they were to call their colleagues so that they could swoop back in to arrest me.

But would I return? Or, once again, was I going to be too smart for them?

That remained to be seen. I'm capable of a lot of things, but accurately predicting the future is not one of them. For now, all I know is what happened in the past.

I was once the partner of Drew Devlin, a popular and well-respected man.

I was a doctor's wife and I almost had it all.

Then I was told a lie and I guess you could say things spiralled out of control from there.

Things are very different now that Drew is no longer around.

Things are very different now that I am the doctor's widow.

PART ONE

BEFORE THE POLICE CAME

ONE

FERN

My freshly manicured nails look pretty as my hands rest on top of the leather steering wheel in my brand-new car. As I wait for the lights to turn green ahead of me, I glance through my driver's side window and see a few pedestrians scurrying past on the busy street, all of them eager to get to wherever they're going, though one thing is for sure.

They won't get there as quickly as I will.

As the cars in front move on, I gently tap the accelerator pedal and I'm back on the move again, gliding through Manchester city centre in the car that I only received the keys for a week ago. But it's the set of keys I am on my way to collect today that I'm really excited about, because while the novelty of my new mode of transport might be starting to wear off a little bit, it will take a lot longer before I grow bored of the stunning house I am about to move into.

The sunlight that has been glinting against the side of some of the taller towers in this city briefly hits my windscreen before I'm back in the shadow of one of those buildings, moving on through the congested area where, all around me, so many people are trying to get to work. It's a time like this that I remember to feel grateful that I don't have to commute, nor do I have to spend most of my week answering to somebody else and patiently waiting for a payslip to be sent to me at the end of the month. That gratitude I feel could have easily worn off by now, seeing as it has been a long time since I was in employment, but it hasn't and, hopefully, it never will.

Drew Devlin is the reason I was able to give up work. That handsome doctor came into my life unexpectedly, swept me off my feet and put a ring on my finger; and after getting me down the aisle, he told me to quit my job and relax because, on his salary, money was no issue. He was right, and throughout the first few years of our marriage, I greatly enjoyed being the doctor's wife and all the perks that came with it. The parties. The holidays. The respectful look on people's faces when Drew told them what he did for a living, while I stood beside him, my arm interlinked with his and smiling, because out of all the women in the world, I was the one who had snared this impressive man. I was happy being myself – Fern Devlin – a wife, a friend, an innocent and honest member of society. I never asked him to cheat on me with Alice. I never asked to move to Arberness, the place he proposed we move to because *she* had gone there first. I certainly never asked for all the dark and destructive thoughts of revenge that came to my mind as a result of all that. But now Drew is gone, leaving me alone after his untimely death four months ago.

However.

I am doing even better as the doctor's widow than I was as the doctor's wife.

As I catch sight of the high-end estate agency ahead through my windscreen, my eyes scan the populated street for a parking space. Anyone looking to leave their vehicle here would normally have to pay a quite extortionate rate for a parking ticket, or else risk the wrath of an overzealous ticket inspector, but, as always, I have a way of getting around the law. That's because, as a client of the estate agency, I am eligible to park in the spot right outside the entrance that is reserved for paying customers, and I'm certainly paying. The amount of money that has left my bank account today could have paid for parking tickets for everyone in this city for the next year.

Hopping out of my stylish Mercedes, I make my way to the entrance wearing an equally stylish outfit – a red poppy jacquard dress matched with a pair of high heels and a designer handbag – which elicits a couple of admiring glances from the two women I pass on my way to the door. Pushing the button on my keyfob that automatically locks my car, I drop that key into my handbag before entering the estate agency in great anticipation of receiving another key. As I smile at the fetching receptionist who welcomes me in, it is clear she has been expecting me.

'Right this way, Mrs Devlin,' the fair-haired young woman says, and I follow her, feeling slightly envious of her smooth skin because she is at least ten years younger than I am, though I'm sure she feels just as envious of me and the property I am here to officially take ownership of.

I get the feeling that she's not the only one; as we pass several desks in the open-plan part of this office, all those in suits who are seated at them briefly look up from their phones or laptops to watch me walk by, and I'm sure they are all thinking the same thing.

Instead of just selling these aspirational homes all day, I wish I could live in one of them myself.

While I'm sure these employees are well compensated via commissions for the stellar work they do in selling expensive homes all over this city, it's the man in the private office at the back of this agency that I am on my way to see today, because he is the one who is earning all the commission on my juicy house sale. His name is Keegan and, as he looks up from his desk to see his latest client enter the room, a wide grin spreads across his chiselled face.

'Mrs Devlin. What a pleasure as always. And right on time, thank you for being so prompt!'

He is quickly out from behind his mahogany desk with his right hand extended towards me, and I shake it before he offers me a seat and asks if there is anything he can get me by way of refreshment. But I just thank him and say I've already had my caffeine quota for the day, so coffee is off the menu for me if I want to get some sleep tonight.

'Okay, how about some champagne?' Keegan suggests, surprising me, and he proves that it wasn't just a joke when he opens the small fridge in the corner of his office, with a bottle sitting in there for an occasion like this.

'Oh, no thank you. I'm driving,' I reply, deciding not to mention that once I have the keys to my new house and have gone inside, popping a bottle of champagne is the first thing on my to-do list. I also forgo mentioning that I'd rather do this without Keegan's company as opposed to with it.

'Right, well let's get you sorted so we don't delay you any longer,' Keegan says as he sits back down, smoothing out the black tie that sits over his crisp white shirt as he does. 'The funds have been received and everything has been processed at our end, which means there are only a couple of things to do and we'll have you on your way.'

Sliding a piece of paper across the desk towards me, Keegan asks me to have a quick read of what is written on it before I sign it; while I do that, he opens his desk drawer and takes out the silver key that I can't wait to have in my hands. But, before I receive it, I do as he says, reading the document and getting confirmation of what I have just paid to own.

FairView Manor, Foxgreen Crescent, Hale, Manchester –
£975,000

Quickly reading through the legal jargon underneath the name of the property I'm purchasing, I see that it is just about me confirming that the estate agency conducted all that was required of them to help me during the sale. That's why I'm happy to pick up the blue fountain pen on Keegan's desk and sign on the dotted line at the bottom. With that, there's only one thing left to do.

'Here you go, Mrs Devlin. Congratulations, and I hope you enjoy your new home.'

The key feels slightly cool to the touch as I receive it. It's almost as cool as I felt inside when I got the key to my previous house, which was many miles north of here, in the picturesque village of Arberness, just south of the Scottish border. I felt cold that day because I knew I was only moving house to appease my husband and I couldn't help but feel, ultimately, it was going to be a bad move for all concerned. But I did it anyway, things played out as they did, and here I am. I'm moving on from Doctor Drew Devlin and feeling much better about this next chapter of my life.

'Thank you for all your help,' I say to Keegan with a big smile on my face. 'I'll be sure to recommend you to any friends who might be looking to move house in the future.'

Keegan appreciates that and thanks me as he shows me to the door. After striding confidently back through the busy office, I step out onto the street and am almost ready to be on my way. But it's just as I'm rummaging around in my handbag for the car key that I hear my phone ringing and, when I check the caller ID, I see the name on screen.

Roger.

It's yet another reason to smile on this day that is turning out to be perfect so far, and I'm happy to delay the journey to my new house by a couple of minutes just to hear from the newest man in my life.

'Hey,' I say breezily as I answer the call.

'Good morning, beautiful. How are you today? Did everything go okay at the estate agents?'

Roger's voice, and his words, fill me with pleasure. He calls me beautiful. He checks up to see how my day is going. And he has remembered that I had an appointment at this estate agency today. In other words, he gives a damn about me.

Too bad for my previous partner that he wasn't the same.

'I'm great. I've just picked up the key this very minute,' I reply as I look down at the small and shiny object in my hand.

'Fantastic! A congratulations is in order! How about I take you out for a drink tonight to celebrate?'

I love the suggestion, but I have an even better one.

'A drink would be good but let's not go out. I want to enjoy my new house tonight. Care to join me and help me enjoy it even more?'

Roger cannot miss a suggestive hint like that one and eagerly accepts my invitation, telling me he will be at my new place as soon as he finishes work for the day, and that he can't wait to see me. I don't doubt that as I end the call, because as interesting as his working day might be, it's surely not as interesting as joining me to drink champagne and engaging in other enjoyable activities later on.

With even more of a spring in my step than when I left my car a few minutes ago, I get back inside and drive away from the designated parking spot, giving the ticket inspector at the end of the street a wave as I pass him because he won't be issuing me with any punishments today. Then I drive through the city, thinking about how I've escaped punishment over several other things in my time and they are far worse things than not paying for a parking space.

It's strange because the old adage says that crime doesn't pay.

If only the person who came up with that one knew the truth.

It sure has paid off for me, and I have the brand-new house to prove it.

TWO

GREG

As a salesman, I make a lot of phone calls in a day. But it's the latest one that is still playing on my mind as I struggle to return my thoughts to work matters. That's because that last call had nothing to do with my job, or at least not the job I'm being paid to do. Instead, it was more about keeping in character as 'Roger', the alias I have assumed as I continue in my quest to unearth the truth about Fern, the ex-wife of my old friend Drew.

I put the phone down on my desk and lean back in my cheap office chair. It's rare that I'm at my desk because I spend most of the week driving around all over the north-west of England to visit clients, but today is supposed to be a 'lead generating' day. That means I should be making business calls now, setting up meetings and doing all I can to close some deals for my employer, as I get paid on commission, not on salary. However, I am not doing that. I'm thinking about Fern and how in a few hours from now, I'm expected to sip champagne with her and compliment her on her beautiful new house.

A house I believe she has purchased with blood money.

Hearing about the death of Drew, a man I played tennis with on several occasions, and who had become a close friend before he abruptly left Manchester to start a new life in Arberness, was more than upsetting. I was aware the popular doctor had a wide and very full social circle, but I have never been known for having lots of friends. That's why I cherished the relationship I had with Drew; I looked forward to our weekly games of tennis, as well as the male bonding time we had in the pub afterwards. I never bothered him on the weekends, well aware that he was likely to be at some dinner party with other doctors and people I might struggle to fit in with, but that was okay. One or two evenings during the week to catch up on the court was fine by me; it gave me the mental break I needed from my own job, as well as the physical exercise a doctor like Drew would surely have prescribed if I was one of his patients. It didn't sadden me to know I was closer to Drew than he was to me; if anything I was just happy to be in his orbit. He had that way with people, charisma, I guess they would call it. I'm sure his wife was just as charmed by him as everyone else he encountered, not that I ever met her. I wouldn't have minded doing so but I wasn't going to suggest it and Drew never invited me to their home. He seemed content with just seeing me as an exercise buddy and I didn't mind that. Men are different to women, aren't they? They don't suddenly become best friends and share intimate details of each other's lives as often as possible. They keep it casual, cool, that's just what men do and that's what Drew and I did.

I do miss him and not just because I haven't set foot on a tennis court since he moved away, and have added an inch or so to my waistline. I miss him because he was not only a nice guy but a consistent presence in my life and, as somewhat of a nomad myself, having a reliable support network of friendly faces I can lean on has not always been an option for me. But while hearing about his death in the news was terrible, what is even more upsetting is being one of the few people in the world who believes there was far more to his death than meets the eye.

The official verdict from the justice system is that Drew was murdered by Alice, a woman he was having an affair with and the woman he had moved to Arberness to be closer to, though, supposedly, nobody else knew about their affair at the time. Not Alice's partner, Rory, and certainly not Drew's partner, Fern. Apparently, the way the prosecution told it, what happened next is that Drew and Alice briefly resumed their affair until Alice decided that she no longer wished to play with fire and betray her partner. She then plotted to kill Drew and remove him from her complicated life. Then, after the body of the village doctor had been found on the beach, and a few incriminating pieces of evidence had been found that linked Alice with the crime, she was arrested and subsequently sentenced to murder after being found guilty by a jury of her peers. Now she is in prison, justice has seemingly been done, and everybody is free to get on with their lives.

But is it that simple?

I let out a deep sigh as I continue to waste even more of my day thinking about Fern. It's a habit that is quickly becoming an obsessive one.

This stuffy spare room in my pokey apartment is a far cry from the trendy wine bar I was in on the night I first encountered Fern Devlin three months ago. While it's currently a very boring Monday, when I met her it was a lively Friday night, as I joined dozens of revellers in that bar to enjoy the beginning of the weekend. However, there was only one reveller I was interested in talking to and, after catching Fern's eye as she sat alone nursing her drink, I introduced myself under a false name and the rest, as they say, is history. We've been dating ever since, although, perhaps rather astutely, Fern has chosen to keep our budding 'romance' secret for the time being. She tells me she is wary of being seen to have moved on from Drew too quickly. Although, as she has also told me, there are no set rules for how a widow must adjust to life by herself, and while some choose to stay alone for years, others wish to move on quickly, to help them deal with the loss and loneliness that can occur. Fern has obviously chosen the latter option and is happy to move on with a new man only a few months after her last one passed away; she says that is how she feels it is best to cope with her grief. But like many things I suspect about that woman, there is far more to all she says and does than first meets the eye. Is she really grieving for Drew or is she actually glad he's gone? Did she know about his affair before his murder, not after it? And is the real reason she hasn't told any of her family or friends about me yet not because she wants to take things slowly but because she is worried people might get a little suspicious if they think her husband's passing has had no negative effect on her?

Those are still uncertainties, but one thing is for sure.

Drew's passing has had some positive effects on her.

One of the biggest of those effects has been the sizeable life insurance policy Fern was given access to once the circumstances around her husband's death had been ironed out in court. I don't know the exact figure she will have received, but considering Drew was a man with a very good job, and also a man who was savvy when it came to things like investments and insurances, I'm sure it's a substantial sum.

It certainly must be based on what his late wife has been buying recently.

A new car. New clothes. New handbags. New nails. That's all before the new house she has just picked the keys up for today, a house that cost an astronomical amount and quite rightly so, because I've seen the photos of it online and it is huge. That's along with its location: it is in a part of the city known for housing many footballers and former pop stars, so it's little wonder why the agency who were tasked with selling it assigned such an eye-watering price tag to the property. Now Fern is the rightful owner, free to enjoy the fruits of Drew's sensible insurance while he lies in a box six feet underground.

That would be all well and good if he had died in circumstances outside of Fern's control, and she would certainly be entitled to every penny if she really was the loyal, loving wife everybody else seems to think she is.

But is she?

While I've spent a lot of time pondering that question over the last few months as I have grown closer to her, I am still no nearer to knowing the definitive answer. I have my suspicions though, simply because of what Drew told me one night after our regular tennis match. After Fern had caught him texting another woman, texting that was completely innocent I might add, she erupted, stunning her husband at the level of anger she was displaying. I think I might be the only person who has heard about that incident between them, as I doubt Fern was in a hurry to share it with friends, which would mean I'm the only one who is aware that Fern has a very jealous streak in her, as well as a temper that can easily get out of control.

I believe that such a streak and temper had something to do with Drew's death, and that's why I'm on the hunt to get the real truth of what happened in Arberness. Until then I just need to remain patient and, most importantly, keep Fern under the belief that I am just some charming guy she met in a bar on a Friday night, who is giving her a little respite from having to think about what she has lost recently.

I can't say I'm enjoying playing the character of 'Roger' and would much prefer to be myself, but being myself is not the best way to get nearer to Fern. If she had known that I was an old acquaintance of her husband's then she would have not allowed me to get as close to her as I have. Especially not if she really does have something to hide about his death, which I believe she does. But, as it is, I have her fooled for now, and that is the way I intend to keep things until I get what I am after, which is any one of two things.

One, evidence of any wrongdoing on her part.

Two, and even better, a confession, given to me after she has completely fallen under my spell and has got no reason not to trust me.

Until that happens, I'll keep playing the role I've been perfecting recently. I'll call and message Fern daily to check in with her and see how she is. I'll tell her how beautiful she is and how I have such a great time when we're together, guaranteeing she'll be happy to keep agreeing to further dates for the two of us. I'll even toast to happy occasions with her like the one she is celebrating today, because pretty soon I'll be clinking a champagne flute against hers before we both sip the cold, fizzy bubbles and comment on how amazing her new house is.

I'll do all those things and so much more if it means getting justice for my late friend. I can't say it's a pleasure to be in Fern's company, not when I suspect her of a heinous crime. Sure, she is interesting, chatty and attractive, all qualities that are no doubt what attracted Drew to her in the first place, but I constantly remind myself that there is more to her than meets the eye. Drew warned me of that and that's why I'm convinced she had something to do with what really occurred in Arberness. It's also why I have to stay on my guard around her. Fern is clever and, while I am too, I am playing a very dangerous game. It's not too dissimilar to the one Drew was playing with Fern. He was keeping a secret from her, just like I am, and that dangerous game turned deadly for him.

Will it do the same for me?

I have to keep pushing that question from my mind if I want to get the truth.

What honestly happened to Doctor Drew Devlin?

The police think they know but I think there's more to it.

The key to getting that answer lies with his widow.

THREE

FERN

The house looks even more magnificent than the last time I saw it as I park on the spacious driveway, which could easily fit another couple of cars on if necessary. But that's surely because last time I was here I was just a prospective buyer.

Now I am the owner.

With the novelty of my new car having worn off and, like a child on Christmas morning, quickly becoming more enamoured with a new, flashy toy rather than the old one that was the former favourite, I waste no time in getting to the front door and putting the key in the lock. As I twist it, I truly know this house is mine now because the door opens easily, and I am free to go inside.

It feels good to be back on the property ladder again, to finally have a new place to truly call home. I've been renting an apartment in the city ever since I returned here after Drew's death but, as all renters know, there's only so much decorating you can do in a place that is owned by somebody else. I've been longing to have somewhere to call my own again, a property I can put my own stamp on, and, here, I have exactly that.

Like the last time I was here when I was accompanied by

Keegan, the first thing that catches my attention is the wide staircase that rises up from the middle of the hallway. I've always wanted a grand staircase like this one, one that is almost a centrepiece in itself. I'm already looking forward to wrapping the bannisters in festive decorations in December, and there is certainly space for a large Christmas tree by the front door that will generate gasps of admiration from all who come to visit me here, at that sociable time of the year.

The room to my right as I enter is what will be the lounge, while the room to my left is going to be the dining room. But it's the room that I can access by walking past the staircase that is my favourite one: the kitchen. It's the kind of kitchen that wouldn't look out of place in a Michelin-starred restaurant. There's so much preparation space with the marble countertops that line the sizeable room, and so many hobs to cook all my meals. There's room for a double fridge as well, not to mention a wine rack, and I'm even entertaining the idea of one part of this kitchen being a designated place where I can bake cakes and bread, my own space to work on just one of the hobbies I am going to get more time to do shortly.

Everything looks as it should be downstairs, so I go upstairs to check on the rooms and find them just as empty and just as ready for me to put my own stamp on them. The master bedroom has room for a king-size bed, and the three spare rooms can each fit a large bed too, although I plan to use one of them for something else. Painting, perhaps. I do have a lot of time on my hands, after all. Then there is the bathroom, a gorgeous piece of architecture with a walk-in shower and even his-and-hers sinks and mirrors. I might be living here alone for the fore-seeable future, but I can still appreciate that touch.

That's not to forget the final feature of this wonderful house. I go outside, to the garden at the rear of the property, and take in the sight of the perfect lawn that is fenced on all sides by luscious green conifers. Those conifers provide a perfect privacy screen between me and the neighbours on all sides, and I'm grateful for that because, while I'm friendly, I don't want people being nosey. I haven't met any of my new neighbours yet, though I am definitely hoping to because, from what I've read about this neighbourhood online, this place is full of celebrities, sports stars and successful entrepreneurs, and that surely has to add up to some very entertaining dinner parties.

The idea of me hosting a dinner party will have to wait for now though, because the first thing I have to do here is furnish this house, but, even before that, there is a little decorating to be done. I plan on having a decorator change the colour scheme in some of these rooms, and I'll require new carpets as well before I have any removal men unload the furniture I currently have in storage. It's furniture that has been moved a lot recently thanks to the two house moves I have done in the past year.

Moving home is a big undertaking and most people like to have many years in between doing such a thing, mainly due to not just how expensive it all is but how stressful it tends to be as well. But I've always had a flair for the dramatic, which might explain why, after leaving Manchester to move to Arberness with Drew, I am now moving back to the city again. All in the space of the same year.

I'm aware that things could have been so very different though. If only Drew hadn't suggested we move up north, then there would've been no need to move at all. And if only he hadn't done what he did when he got to Arberness, there would have been no need for me to move back here by myself after attending his funeral, and faking all those tears I cried during it.

Moving to the village of Arberness had been a necessary evil: I had to test my husband to see if he had changed once I discovered he had been cheating on me in the city. But he failed that test miserably, so here I am, starting afresh once again. Only this time, my future is not in the hands of an untrustworthy man: I am in control. While I might technically be involved with another male at present, it's only a casual thing and nobody else but me and Roger know about it. I'm having fun with him and things may get serious further down the line but, for now, I am keeping him at arm's length, at least figuratively speaking. That's because it's not only still early days since I lost my husband, but also I don't want to quickly dive into another situation in which my happiness is intrinsically linked to somebody else. While it's always good to have a companion, I'm more than capable of being content by myself and, after being married for almost a decade, there's no point rushing into another legal matrimony anytime soon. However, the main reason I'm quite happy to take things slow with Roger and enjoy living here by myself for a while is because I'm aware of one very crucial thing.

Men, or at least ones with bad intentions, seem to bring out the worst in me.

The thing is, a celebratory day like today is not the time for me to be dwelling on the past, so I will push all thoughts of them away for the time being and try to enjoy this.

I'm confident that it will work out for the most part.

It tends to be when I go to sleep that I have a harder time of forgetting about what happened before.

Thankfully, the sun is still up and bedtime is a long way off yet, so I don't worry about any nightmares that might be waiting to welcome me after I've slipped into a slumber. Instead, I get busy calling the removal company who are due to bring a few of my essential items here to help me settle in. While most things will stay in storage for the time being, there are some things I can't do without and those include a bed, a fridge and something to sit on and eat at. After the gruff northerner at the other end of the line tells me the van with those things inside it will be with me within the hour, I get on with my next job, an online food shop, and happily fill my virtual basket with all sorts of tasty treats that will keep me going throughout the first week in my new surroundings.

It sure is nice to be able to order as much as I want from the supermarket without having to worry about the price of it all, and that is just another added benefit of the life insurance policy that paid out upon Drew's demise. At the time my late husband took out the policy, I had honestly told him that even though his death would technically make me an instant millionaire, I'd much rather have him around than have access to a big pile of money but nobody to share it with. But then he went and did what he did with Alice, a woman who must have thought she was better than me until her sins caught up with her; and now I'm perfectly pleased that Drew is dead and I'm left with a fortune that will take me the rest of my life to spend.

I've already made a pretty good start on that front.

It initially occurred to me that I should perhaps limit my spending in the early stages because it might not do me any good to be seen to be enjoying the fruits of my late husband's insurance. What if people thought I was being flash or having too much of a good time to be grieving? I didn't want people gossiping about me, and I certainly didn't want to arouse people's suspicions that I might have somehow manufactured this situation for myself, instead of just being the innocent widow that everyone thought I was. But, after what I'd been through, I realised those fears were unfounded, because everyone who knew me told me that I had to do whatever I could to get through this time, and if that meant buying a nice car or a big house or taking a fancy holiday then so be it. Who were they to judge because they hadn't lost their partner like I had? Having everyone assume that I am suffering greatly on the inside has been a big help in being able to splurge on some of the finer things in life because, to them, I'm just trying to compensate for the aching void that Drew's death left for me to languish in.

That's absolutely fine by me.

I have no regrets about anything that transpired in Arberness, and I gratefully take delivery of both my groceries and my essential furniture items from storage. I did what I had to do back then and I'll continue to do whatever I have to do now to get away with it. Part of that means keeping those close to me happy, because if they think I'm okay then they're less likely to pry into anything that happened before. That's why I take a few photos of my new house and send them to my parents, as well as to a few of my best friends. I want them all to see that I am doing okay and moving on as best I can, and if they think that, they're more likely to go back to being absorbed in their own lives and be less obsessed with mine. I appreciate everyone being worried about me, but enough is enough.

I'm back and I'm feeling better than ever.

As if to prove it even more, I'm pleased when I open the door shortly after 5 p.m. to see my new man standing on my doorstep with a bottle of champagne in one hand and a huge grin across his face.

'Happy moving in day!' Roger says before he leans in to give me a kiss, and I quickly usher him into the house so we can make a start on the bubbly. He's been a real ray of light in my life ever since he approached me in a bar one Friday night not long after I'd moved back to Manchester. To prove just how great he is, he has even remembered to bring two champagne flutes with him, knowing it was unlikely I would have got mine unpacked or even out of storage in time for our toast.

As he pops the cork and pours us both a measure, I can't help but daydream for a moment about how things might go with Roger. One day, a good few months off yet, but possibly sooner than that depending on how I feel, I may ask him if he'd like to move in with me here, and I'm pretty sure what his answer would be. Who can say no to living in a house like this?

Then I'll be back to where I started before all the drama of my past; living in a city I love, in a house I love, with a man I love.

It'll be like Arberness never happened.

It'll definitely be like Drew never happened.

And that is just fine by me.

FOUR

GREG

I can't say it was much fun to sip champagne with Fern and follow her around her brand-new home as she gave me the guided tour. Listening to her harping on about what she planned to do in one of the spare bedrooms, or which colour paint she had earmarked for the walls in the dining room, was hardly riveting stuff for me, made even harder by the fact that I hated her guts and despised the fact she was clearly living well due to her husband's death. If Fern was harbouring any guilt about what she might have done to Drew to speed up the time he had left on this earth, she hid it very well, barely even pausing for breath as she took me from one room to the next and told me all about her grand visions for her new purchase. In fact, the only time she did stop talking for that first hour I was there was when she put her champagne flute to her lips and drank some of the bubbles I had poured for her. At least then I got a little peace.

However, I'd be lying if I said the entire 'housewarming' experience at Fern's was a tough one for me. Once the tour was over and the champagne had started to take effect, particularly on the excitable homeowner because she had far more glasses than I did, we stopped talking and did something else. There isn't much furniture in Fern's new place but there is a bed and that was where we found ourselves before too long.

Yes, I'm sleeping with Fern, which may seem strange considering how much I hate her and can't trust a word she says about what really happened with Drew, but I have to keep up appearances as the new man in her life. I doubt our relationship would get very far if we weren't intimate with one another. In fact, it would get to the point where Fern would think I was strange for not even trying to sleep with her, and I can't have her getting suspicious of me at all. As far as she is to know, I'm just a regular guy she met in a bar and, if that's the case, a regular guy would be more than eager to be physical with a woman who looks like her.

The way I see it, it is just a means to an end, a way of getting close enough to Fern so that she trusts me explicitly. Pillow talk may be the best way to get her to reveal some of her darkest secrets to me, secrets I can expose to the police, but pillow talk can't happen if we're not actually lying on a pillow together. The potent mixture of alcohol along with three post-sex hormones and chemicals as powerful as oxytocin, dopamine and endorphins may eventually be the trigger for Fern to tell me a little too much about her past. It didn't happen this time, but I am confident I can get there, as she clearly has no idea that I am not to be trusted.

I know that for a fact because, just as I was leaving her place tonight, she told me that she was glad I had been the first person she had made a memory with in her new home. It could have been her parents or best friends that she had quaffing champagne with her on night one, but it was me and she said she was happy about that – though still not quite happy enough to let me stay the night.

As well as our relationship – and my continued deception – is going, Fern is still keeping me at a safe distance. One of the ways she is doing that is politely suggesting I leave and go home so we can both get a good night's rest.

While Fern is more than happy to fall into bed with me, she is not so happy to stay in that bed for longer than necessary, and that means as of yet we haven't woken up together the morning after a night of passion, or shared any heartfelt conversations in the early hours of the morning, which is a time when it's most likely I could elicit a confession from her about Drew. But again, I feel it's just a matter of time, so until then, I have been careful not to press the issue and demand that I get to spend the entire night with her, because that might only push her away when my intention is to pull her closer.

I've also made the effort to take things slowly on my part too, not wanting to spook her or push her away before she's ready to get too serious. One of the ways I have done that is by not having her visit my place, and we have kept our dates to mostly public places, bars and restaurants that are more befitting of a couple still in the early stages of a romantic relationship. The one-bedroom apartment is a world away from what Fern is accustomed to, and I'm sure seeing where I live would put her off me a little. She's never intimated anything like that, nor has she explicitly asked to see where I live, so I'm aware she is more than happy to just have me visit her when she wants. That fits nicely into my plan, otherwise I'd have to worry about Fern seeing something in my flat that might have my real name on it, or perhaps a nosy neighbour of mine would poke their head out of their door and say something to her that might go against the lies I've already spun.

A plan as delicate as mine does not need to be blown up by leaving things to chance.

With our goodbyes complete, I drive away from the splendid suburb that Fern now resides in, all the way to the part of the city where property is cheaper and consists more of high-rise apartment blocks and council flats rather than big homes and sprawling gardens on tree-lined streets. Fuelled by a need for the truth about the doctor's widow, as well as the slight buzz from the champagne that by this time has safely worn off to the point where I am okay to drive, I bring my vehicle to a stop in the crowded car park beside the fifteen-storey apartment block I call home.

I take the elevator up to the tenth floor and, after trying to ignore the smell of something quite putrid in the corridor, not to mention the very loud television set behind one of my neighbour's doors, I make it to Flat 1006 and put my key in the lock. As always, the key and the lock have a slight disagreement and it takes me a couple of seconds of wriggling before it unjams and the door releases, but that's just one of the many joys of the place I get to rent for a ridiculous sum of money each month.

Stepping into my humble abode, I take off my suit jacket and toss it onto my small sofa in the 'lounge area' before taking two steps and ending up in my 'kitchen', which consists of nothing more than one countertop, a microwave and a very small fridge that can never hold more than two days' worth of food. Deciding not to disturb the one beer bottle that I have managed to squeeze into the fridge, because it's late and I have to be up early tomorrow, I make my way towards my bedroom, but pause as I go to look at the only thing this place really has going for it.

The view.

Gazing out over the twinkling lights of Manchester at midnight, I think as I often do when standing here about all the people down below and all the lives they are leading. But it never takes long for my thoughts to focus on one particular resident of this city, and after trying and failing to figure out which one of the many lights out there on the landscape belongs to Fern's new property, I carry on into the bedroom. It's not exactly easy to forget about her in here either, and that is thanks to the rudimentary wallchart I have made and stuck to one of the walls. It consists of various things linked to Fern's past and proves that I am on the trail for the truth.

There are photos here of all the key pawns in the dangerous game Fern has played. There's Drew, of course, the late doctor who paid the ultimate price for betraying his wife. There is Alice, the beautiful mistress who played with fire when she began an affair with Drew and ultimately paid the price as well when, as I believe, she was framed for his murder by Fern. There's also Rory, Alice's partner, who died after apparently falling asleep in his bathtub at home while drunk, presumably having drowned his sorrows over Alice's conviction, and all she had done, before literally drowning his sorrows in the tub. Considering Rory passed away in Arberness on the same night Fern left the quiet village for good, I'm almost certain she had something to do with his demise too. I expect she was tying up a loose end, a loose end no doubt linked to the plot that saw Drew die and Alice go to prison for his murder.

There is also a photo up on this wall of Detective Tomlin, the man who was in charge of Drew's murder investigation and, ultimately, the detective who believed he had served justice when he charged Alice with the crime and watched on in court as she was sentenced to twenty years for it. I have thought about making contact with him on a couple of occasions, so I can share with him my theory that Fern might actually be the guilty party after all, but I have so far stopped myself because I don't want to risk the detective telling Fern that there is some madman running around trying to prove some crazy idea about her. I will have to speak to him soon, though, as he holds a lot of information about the case, and it would be helpful if somebody else was aware of what I'm doing. That way, if Fern tries to stop me at any point, someone else can pick up the investigation.

The only time I have spoken to anybody in the police about

Fern and how I think she has managed to get away with murder was when I contacted a couple of my old colleagues in the police force. I used to be a servant of that same force myself. I left after becoming worn down by life upholding law in this crime-ridden country. But none of them seemed interested in anything I had to say, and I could hardly blame them, because as I knew all too well from my past in the police, without evidence, there is nothing they could do. So far, the only evidence in Drew's murder points to Alice, which is why she is the one in a pokey prison cell while Fern is the one in a humongous home.

But we'll see about that.

After wearily getting undressed and brushing my teeth in my bathroom that I can only just fit in, I fall into bed and try to get some rest. However, lying in the dark and listening to the sounds coming from not only the flats around me but also from the busy inner-city streets below, it's hard not to question my life choices. I've gone from being a fairly well-paid policeman to scraping a living as a salesman. On top of that, I've become obsessed with proving the guilt of a woman that everyone else thinks is innocent.

I guess you can take the man out of the police force but not the police out of the man.

Perhaps it was inevitable that I would find something to drag me back into my old way of life, something to sink my investigative teeth into and keep me up late at night running through various theories and scenarios in my head. It seems to be just the way I'm wired; I need a problem to solve or, rather, I need an injustice to set right. All this cloak and dagger stuff with Fern, this reality of acting independently and trying to unearth key truths and information might be what's making me consider what could come after this. Maybe the right move for me career-wise would be to set up my own private investigative firm. I might not be getting paid to do what I'm doing now, but I can be good at it so why not try and make a living from it? Doing such a thing would give me the best of both worlds. I'd still get to do what I feel I do naturally, which is trying to solve crime, but without all the constraints and demands of being employed by any branch of the police. I'd be fully free, a PI for hire, marching to the sound of my own drum and bending whatever rules I need to bend in order to get what I want, rather than worrying about falling into line alongside all my other uniformed officers.

That's all stuff to think about in the future though. For now, this is my first assignment and it's far from over yet. I don't even know if it will reach a satisfactory conclusion, and that wouldn't bode well for securing clients in the future.

What if I'm wrong?

What if Fern didn't really conspire with Rory to kill Drew, frame Alice and then kill Rory when it was all done?

What if all of this is a waste of time?

Facing that reality is daunting, but, on the other hand, the alternative is even more frightening.

What if I'm right?

What if Fern is a killer?

Most importantly, what if she figures out what I'm doing and kills me next?

FIVE

FERN

I've tried to stay up as late as I can since Roger left but it's past midnight now and my eyelids are growing heavy after what has been a very busy day. The champagne is also contributing to my drowsiness, not to mention the comedown I am experiencing after all the good feelings of intimacy with my new man start to wear off.

It's no good. I'm going to have to close my eyes and get some sleep.

All I can hope is that, tonight, the nightmares stay away.

It's frustrating that after taking care of business so precisely in Arberness, and moving back to Manchester without being under suspicion by anybody, I have recently been plagued with all sorts of bad dreams and flashbacks about what I had to do to get to this position. It's frustrating because, while I don't feel guilty in the daytime, my subconscious sure seems to feel that way in the night-time, and there's very little I can do about it if I want to get some sleep. Some nights are okay, but there are others where I wake up drenched in sweat and, on rare occasions, wake up screaming. That's not ideal and another reason why I have not yet let Roger spend the entire night with me.

It wouldn't look good if he was beside me in bed when I suffered another distressing episode. He'd ask me what could be causing it and I can hardly be honest with him.

I spoke to a doctor about the nightmares and was able to get a prescription for some sleeping tablets, which sometimes knock me out enough to the point where very little can stir me from my slumber until dawn. I told the doctor that, after losing my husband to a heinous crime, I was understandably struggling with visions of the awful things that happened to him, and the man with the prescription pad was very sympathetic to my plight.

I guess you could say he was a very naïve doctor.

Just like the last doctor I knew.

However, the tablets are not a cure for any bad dreams I might have and, as I drift off to sleep after taking a couple of them, I am praying that the next time I open my eyes, I will see sunlight streaming through the luxurious curtains that the previous owner kindly left behind in this master bedroom. That will mean I have safely made it through until dawn without being pulled from my slumber by some awful vision.

But that remains to be seen.

'How was your day?'

The familiar male voice behind me gives me a surprise. I wasn't expecting anybody but, as I turn around from the pile of empty boxes on the countertop, I see Drew entering the kitchen, looking sharp in a suit and with a carefree grin on his face.

'What are you doing home? It's the middle of the afternoon,' I say, confused as to why my husband is here and not at his surgery caring for one of his patients.

'Julie had to leave early and I can't keep working without my receptionist, so we closed for the day,' Drew says as he takes a

beer from the fridge, intent on making a good start to his free afternoon.

But I have other ideas.

'Great, you can help me with some of this unpacking,' I tell him, gesturing to the multitude of boxes all around the room that have been keeping me busy ever since we got to Arberness and moved into this house.

'I thought we could do something a little more fun than that,' Drew replies, and the suggestive expression tells me exactly what he has in mind.

But is he feeling frisky because he wants to be with me?

Or is it because he is desperately craving Alice, and, as she hasn't given him what he wants, he has to get his fun elsewhere for the time being?

Maybe if I was feeling more focused I would be able to resist his charms, but I'm feeling a little lightheaded for some reason, almost as if I'm in a trance, and that means I am powerless to prevent Drew getting closer to me. He's close enough now to run his hands over my body, hands that spend most of the day writing on prescription pads, taking blood pressure checks and poking around patients' bodies to locate any areas that might be feeling tender. But his hands are only caring for me now.

I have the full attention of the doctor.

Just like it always used to be.

Before her.

And I'm loving it.

I'm loving it as we go upstairs to the bedroom and while away an hour, rolling around amongst all the empty boxes that we haven't unpacked yet since we uprooted our lives in Manchester and moved to this village.

I wake up with a start and feel a few beads of sweat on my forehead, and, as I look around my new bedroom, I realise it was just another dream about Drew. But, unlike many of the recent dreams, that was actually quite a pleasant one. Or at least it was while I was in it and he was kissing my lips and caressing my skin. Now that I'm awake, I shudder at the memory of my late husband and how those lips and hands of his spent as much time on his mistress as they did on me.

I want to go back to sleep but I feel I need to reset, so I get up and go to my bathroom, my spacious bathroom with the his-and-hers sinks. It's still dark outside so I have to be careful where I'm going, but I've also committed to not turning any lights on because I want to be able to get back to sleep quickly after this.

After using the toilet, I stand in front of one of the sinks and wash my hands. As I turn off the tap, I expect to hear the sound of running water cease. But that's not what happens. While my tap is off, I realise the one in the sink a couple of yards to my right is running.

How can that be so?

Then I see why.

It's because Drew is standing at it and smiling at me.

Quick as a flash, I reach out for the bathroom light and turn it on and, when I do, Drew has gone. It must have been my imagination playing tricks on me in the dark. I guess that serves me right for creeping around my new house in the middle of the night when I have so much on my mind. Time to go back to bed; hopefully, this time there will be no dreams at all.

But before I go, I take one last look in the mirror in front of me.

That's when I see Drew's bloodied face staring right back at me.

This time, I wake up screaming and it's only after I have calmed down that I realise I hadn't woken up at all after the first dream. I was still asleep and that explains why I just saw my late husband in the bathroom. Of course he's not really here, because he is dead and I am miles away from where he died in Arberness. Although that doesn't mean I feel comforted as I look around my dark bedroom to doublecheck there are no more surprises for me. Thankfully, there aren't.

I really am awake now. I'm also not in any rush to go back to sleep in case anything like that happens again. Instead, I pick up my phone from the bedside table and use it to browse the internet, a tried and tested timewasting tactic when a person is awake in the night and has little else to do.

While I spend the first ten minutes or so reading news articles about people I don't know personally, I soon find myself typing in the names of people I did know. Names like Drew Devlin. Alice Richardson. Rory Richardson. Detective Tomlin of Cumbria Constabulary. These are all people I like to read about online, if only to make sure there are no recent news stories on them. If there were, it would worry me that the cases that should be closed might not be as closed as I thought. But all the articles I find about these people are ones I've read in the past, so that tells me nothing new has happened recently and that is just the way I like it.

Satisfied that my secret remains buried and is only likely to stay that way the more time that passes, I put my phone back down. But I don't close my eyes this time. I just stare at the curtains until the darkness disappears on the other side of them and I know it is morning then. It's been another bad night's sleep but at least I don't have to go to work. All I have to do today is enjoy my first full day inside my amazing new home and that should make handling my fatigue easier.

It would be far worse to be tired in a place that wasn't so nice as this.

A place like prison.
A place full of criminals.
A place where an innocent person does not belong.
Now that would truly be awful.
Thankfully, that's not my problem.
It's hers.

SIX

ALICE

The door to my cell gets unlocked at 7.45 a.m. each morning, but I'm always awake long before then. That's because it's nigh on impossible to sleep through the night in prison. There are too many sounds coming from the prisoners in the other cells. Moaning, groaning, cries for help, pleas of innocence or angry threats. It's always noisy and, despite wrapping my pillow around my head many times during the night to cover my ears, it's hard to drown it all out.

But I always stay quiet. I don't cry out in the night or demand that a prison warden come and see me, even though I have plenty of reason to: I shouldn't be in here and I deserve to be released immediately. I keep myself to myself as best I can, as I was warned by another inmate on the first day I came here that's the best way a person survives in a place as dangerous as this.

If it wasn't daunting enough to be sentenced for a crime I didn't commit, it was certainly daunting to enter an environment in which it was clear very early on that I was going to have to be on my guard the whole time in case anybody wished me harm. As a convicted killer, which would be laughable if it wasn't so frightening, I am now forced to co-exist with murderers and, unlike me, they are people who have actually taken another person's life.

While I did not kill Doctor Drew Devlin and should not be here, the other inmates have done the things they have been accused of and, in many cases, they are proud to admit it. I'll never forget meeting the inmate known as Chezza on my second day, and hearing about how she murdered her parents to speed up the process of receiving her inheritance from them and, when she was caught, she openly admitted what she had done and told the police she had no regrets. I can't quite comprehend how a person could not only kill someone but then not regret it afterwards. In many ways, I am in the minority here.

As I lie on my very uncomfortable mattress with my head on a pillow that is almost as flat as a pancake, I think about what will happen when my door is unlocked around an hour from now. As is the case with most people, the first thing to do is eat breakfast, but I won't be walking into a nice kitchen and tucking into freshly squeezed orange juice and a plate of eggs and bacon, or putting a little jam onto a croissant and taking a bite of the tasty, flaky pastry. Instead, I'll be getting in line to receive a bowl of porridge and a dry piece of toast with everyone else here before taking a seat at one of the many long tables in the canteen area and eating in silence.

The only time I might talk is if I end up sitting next to the one person who I could potentially refer to as a friend in here. That would be Siobhan, an Irish woman who is serving an eight-year sentence for the attempted murder of her ex-boss. She maintains that she only did what she did because he was treating her unfairly, and while that might have been so, it surely didn't give her the right to poison the poor guy and leave him in hospital, hooked up to all sorts of machines for several months as he clung on to life. But despite taking that drastic approach to dealing with her former employer, Siobhan is otherwise a nice enough person, or at least she has been nice to me. No one else but Siobhan has looked out for me in here. She is the one who gave me the advice to keep myself to myself on my first day and, since then, she has been the only one who asks me how I am and tries to cheer me up occasionally with funny stories about the kinds of things she got up to growing up in Ireland.

Unfortunately for me, Siobhan's sentence is due to end soon and she will be released shortly after, well before me. It's good news for her but it means my one ally in this awful place will no longer be around to look out for me.

And an ally is something I could do with considering I already seem to have an enemy in this place.

Her name is Kelly and while she is also a blonde woman in her late thirties, that is where the similarities between us ends. That's because while I've spent my life trying to be a law-abiding citizen, and I hope to get out, Kelly has had no problems committing numerous crimes at any opportunity, which is why she is expected to spend the rest of her life in prison. Murder, assault and blackmail are just some of the things Kelly has had a go at in her time, and though she hasn't been good enough at any of them to avoid ending up behind bars, she is good enough to scare everybody in here into doing what she says. Technically, it is the wardens who run this prison wing but, in reality, Kelly is the one who rules the roost. A prisoner here is far better just doing what she wants them to do rather than risk facing her wrath.

The last person who defied Kelly was apparently taken out of here in a body bag.

Unfortunately, Kelly never even gave me a chance because she took an instant dislike to me as soon as I was brought in, and, though I haven't done anything to aggravate her, she has only shown aggression towards me ever since. Siobhan thinks it is because of my good looks and the fact that I do not look at all like any of the other women in here. That might be so, but I hardly feel like I'm a glamorous prisoner, because I have no access to makeup and my uniform is just as dull and dreary as the one everyone else is wearing. That hasn't stopped Kelly from targeting me, and after threatening me with violence for several days over the last few weeks, she finally got her hands on me over the weekend, long enough to give me a black eye. I'd hoped the wardens would have done more to punish her than what they actually did but, in the end, they just sent each of us back to our cells as if we were both in the wrong. I knew better than to try and put them right though, as the only thing worse than being an innocent person in prison is being a 'grass', the kind who tells tales on the other prisoners to those in authority to try and get them in trouble. So I kept my mouth shut and have patiently been allowing my bruise to heal since then. I'm also praying Kelly leaves it at that; if she doesn't, I'm not sure how long I could survive in this place.

Assuming I make it through breakfast okay, the next part of my day will involve me working and that means six hours of cleaning. It could be in the canteen, it could be in a vacant cell or it could be in the laundrette. Wherever it is, I'll be on my hands and knees scrubbing a floor with a wet sponge until I get told to stop. It's a far cry from the life I had before everything was turned upside down and I came to this prison in Carlisle. I was living in Arberness, a peaceful village with fantastic views, nice shops and friendly locals. I was living there with Rory, my husband, and I had expected to grow old in the pleasant surroundings, enjoying my time while Rory worked his IT job in the day and went for a beer in the village pub in the evening. But fate transpired against me, and I was followed to that village by the man I had been having an affair with in Manchester.

I couldn't believe it when Drew turned up in Arberness, particularly when I discovered he had started in the role of the new village doctor, meaning his presence there was going to be permanent. I had been trying to get away from him and end our affair, and he knew, as I'd made it clear to him. But he found me and, when he did, he was able to put me under his spell once again.

I'm not proud of the fact I cheated on Rory with Drew, but even though I made mistakes in my marriage, that was all I did wrong. At no point did I do anything that warranted ending up in a cell like this with killers like Kelly for company.

The initial period after Drew's death was a tough one for me. Not only was it a shock to hear that his body had been found on the beach one morning by a dogwalker, it was also confirmation that I would never see that man again. Drew had his faults, as did I, and there is no doubt that him not reappearing in my life again would have made my life easier, but I wouldn't have wished what happened to him on anybody. Who deserves to get bludgeoned over the head with a hard object and left to bleed out on the sand on a freezing cold winter's night?

Kelly perhaps.

And there's one other person I can think of who would have deserved such a fate.

The person who framed me for Drew's murder.

It was all a whirlwind once the doctor's body had been found and the police began their investigation into his death, and it continued to be a whirlwind when I was taken into custody and questioned about my possible involvement in it. Things were just as crazy and fast paced when I was charged and then summoned to court. I tried to defend myself and to convince a judge and jury that I had nothing to do with what happened to Drew, but I was found guilty and marched away in handcuffs to begin my sentence here. Things happened so quickly that I barely had time to figure out how any of it was happening. I had naively assumed justice would be done and the police would realise their mistake. But that never happened and, once I was locked up, time seemed to come to a standstill. Since then, I have had plenty of hours to think about things, and that is how I have come up with my best guess as to what must have happened for me to be charged with Drew's murder.

Rory must have done it. He must have killed him. As my husband, he certainly had a strong motive to do so because I was sleeping with Drew, and that would have struck at the heart of any loyal partner. Rory told the police that he had no idea about our affair until after the doctor had died and the messages on mine and Drew's phones showed we had been romantically involved. I'm not sure I believe that any more. Rory must have known sooner and he must have taken his revenge on the pair of us, killing Drew and framing me for it.

Why am I so convinced of that? It's because Rory died a short time after my conviction.

Having got drunk in the village pub, he went home alone, fell asleep in the bathtub and drowned. I believe he drank so much and put himself in a perilous position because he was guilty about what he had done and, feeling unable to live with it but not wanting to own up for his crime and go to prison, he slipped beneath the water, leaving me as the last one standing to take the fall for it all.

That has to be it, doesn't it? I can't see how anything else could have happened. Who else could have murdered Drew and used my phone to frame me by telling the doctor where to be on the night he was killed? Unfortunately, nobody who will listen to me believes my story, barring Siobhan of course, and, even then, I think she might just be being polite; after all, I'm not the first convicted criminal to insist that they are innocent and have been wronged. The police certainly don't believe me. Not Detective Tomlin or anybody else involved in the investigation. They're all convinced the case is closed, and that's no good to me now because they are the only people who can help me.

There are a few people who have written to me since I have

been in prison, and while some of them tell me they are on my side and think there is more to the story of Drew's death than meets the eye, none of them have any power whatsoever to overturn the jury's decision. I appreciate their support, even if some of them are most likely just lonely on the outside world and find writing to a prisoner is easier than talking to somebody in real life. I wouldn't be the first person serving a prison sentence to receive fan mail, and I'm certainly famous enough to get some considering my picture was all over the front pages of the newspapers when I was on trial. But apart from one guy called Greg, whose letters of support to me are quite sweet, everyone else seems like a bit of a loon. Even Greg can't help me: he's just a civilian and I need a police officer on my side.

Unfortunately, the police have moved on. But I can't move on. How can I?

I can't do so until justice is done, and I am freed.

The problem is, I have no idea how to make that happen.

SEVEN

FERN

It's the first Friday night in my new house and I've decided to host a housewarming party befitting this incredible property. Having had a few days to unpack and either place old furniture where I want it or purchase new furniture to experiment with, this place is starting to look a lot more lived in and, dare I say, starting to feel like home.

In the dining room there's a stylish wooden table and chairs. I've got a beautiful new rug for the lounge, and the kitchen cupboards are now filled with a mixture of old and new utensils, all of which are gleaming, fresh out of the dishwasher that arrived and was installed yesterday by a man with lots of tattoos. Perhaps most importantly, the fridge is almost overflowing with items conducive to a housewarming party, from bottles of champagne, white wine and prosecco, to cheeses, olives and calorific dips that are sure to send everyone who indulges in them scurrying to the gym first thing tomorrow morning, to work off all those extra calories. Everyone except me because I'm making sure not to overeat. I don't have time for running on a treadmill or lifting a few weights anytime soon. I still have a lot to do around this place and, as if on cue, one of my friends, Claire, reminds me of that.

'What are you thinking of doing in here?' she asks me as the two of us, along with another two of my friends, stand at the bottom of the impressive staircase and look around it.

'I'm going to have this carpet pulled up and the steps varnished,' I say.

'Oh, I love staircases like that. Makes it feel more rustic.'

'Yeah, then I'll have a runner down the centre of the staircase and paint the wooden parts grey. Hang a couple of paintings on the wall. Maybe put a small cupboard by the front door. I also want to replace the door at some point. I'm thinking black.'

It sounds like I have it all mapped out in my mind, and I do. Then again, the same could be said of everything in my life, not just renovating and decorating.

'It's going to look amazing,' Claire tells me and the rest of the women agree before we all move into the lounge, where we find their partners relaxing on the sofas with a glass of red wine in their hands and a few snacks on the coffee table between them.

It could feel awkward for me to have several couples here so soon after the loss of my own partner, but I am determined not to let such a fact lower the mood, because I want everybody here to have a great time this evening. To ensure that good time continues, I put on a little music, nothing too heavy, just some background noise to break through any occasional silences, not that there will be any. I'm confident about that because these people are all good friends of mine and we know each other well, having been close for several years now.

There is Claire and her husband, Phil. He's a doctor and used to work with Drew at a surgery across the city when they were younger. I got on with Claire as soon as I met her, the pair of us bonding quickly over the fact we were both doctor's wives.

While the men were often busy discussing health studies they had recently read about, we would bond over the fact we were both married to men with such a respectable profession. In here alongside them is Aimee and Clark and, of the two of them, it's Aimee who is the doctor. Drew and I met them at a medical charity gala five years ago, after we were seated at the same table, and we got on so well that we became firm friends who have even holidayed together a couple of times in the past. The skiing trip that the four of us took to France in 2019 was a particular highlight, although the part where I thought I'd broken my arm at one point after taking a fall on the slopes was not. However, being the medical professionals amongst us, both Drew and Aimee assured me that I would be okay and they were right. The pain quickly subsided, which was a combination of their correct diagnosis as well as all the wine I enjoyed back at the chalet that evening.

Last but not least, there is Chris and Adam, a couple of guys Drew and I actually helped get together. I knew Chris from a Pilates class I used to go to, while Drew knew Adam from medical school, and, after witnessing them both struggle to find love, we set them up on a date and they've been together ever since. They're even thinking about adopting now, which will be wonderful for them and whichever lucky child they eventually end up welcoming into their home.

Many of these people have connections to Drew and the medical profession, but I don't mind that because, as well as enjoying their company, I do still wish to mingle in a few of the social circles that I became used to when married to a doctor. The decadent dinner parties. The glitzy galas. The champagne and canape-fuelled charity functions. Just because there is no longer a doctor in my bed every night, it doesn't mean I don't want to mingle with those in the profession and maintain the lifestyle I was accustomed to before my marriage went a little off track, to put it mildly.

However, being the odd one out in the room, the only one to be flying solo now without a loving companion by my side, while not awkward for me, is proving to be slightly delicate for everyone else in attendance this evening. Nobody makes it obvious, as they are all far too polite and socially conscious to do that, but there are little hints of it every now and again, little moments where my friends can't help but say something that ultimately reminds everybody else here of the metaphorical elephant in the room.

Drew was murdered.

I am now alone.

And, presumably, they are all happy in their lives while I am still grieving.

While I wouldn't consider myself the grieving widow at all, I must keep up appearances, so I am making sure not to be overly fun tonight, smiling when I should and chatting as often as I can, but also keeping a lid on things, just so nobody could ever accuse me of not acting in the manner in which a woman who has recently lost her husband should. But I'd say it's more difficult for the other people here, because they end up having to tiptoe around certain subjects and walk on eggshells, as it were, as various topics that we usually talk about are brought up. Topics like holidays, for example.

Claire and Phil tell us all about a trip to South Africa they have booked for the end of next month. It's a location that draws a few envious gasps from the other guests here when it is mentioned, before lots of questions are asked about what the holidaymakers plan to do while they are in that particular country. However, while Claire and Phil do discuss a few of their plans, I can sense they are also avoiding overplaying how excited they are, surely because they know that I've just lost my holiday partner and it will most likely be a long time before I'm flying off somewhere exotic to go sightseeing with another person by my side.

The topic of Aimee and Clark's ten-year wedding anniversary comes up too at one point, and while Aimee tells us all what she and her partner of a decade have planned to mark the momentous occasion, she quickly stops talking when she sees me take a large gulp from my glass of wine, surely because she fears I might be struggling to listen to something like that. Little does she know, I was taking a large gulp of wine because I'm feeling fantastic and want to keep doing so, but better she believes it's the former, not the latter.

Finally, there is the tender subject of parenthood that comes up when Claire asks Chris and Adam how their foray into adoption is progressing. However, while I've been easily able to feel non-plussed about the other things that have been discussed so far here tonight, this is where I do actually feel awkward myself. That's because, as the date of my fortieth birthday is almost upon me, I am well aware that time is running out if I was to have any offspring of my own.

It was never something I felt hugely worried about before, but that's probably because Drew and his affair kept me busy over the past year or so and, before that, I was naively revelling in still being comfortable inside my thirties and feeling like most do at that age, in so much as that I'd be young forever and growing old was just something that happened to other people. But as Chris and Adam talk about some of the legal hoops they are having to jump through in order to progress their right to adopt a child, who would fill the only void they currently have in their otherwise happy lives, I feel a pang of regret nipping at my insides.

What if I could have been a mum? Would I have been a good one? What would my child have been like?

Maybe being a good mother could have redeemed all the bad things I have done in my past?

I feel like I'm doing a good job of disguising my sudden bout of melancholy and pensive thoughts by staying quiet and half-listening to Chris and Adam's adoption chatter. But perhaps I'm doing too good of a job of it because Claire picks up on the fact that I haven't said a single word for several minutes, and then I see her ever so discreetly give Adam a nudge on his leg, and I realise she is politely indicating to him that he should perhaps shut up chattering about children when there is a widow in the room, who may have lost her last chance at parenthood herself now she has buried her husband.

'So, tell us, Fern!' Claire exclaims, trying to be overly excited and change the subject as quickly as she can. 'What do you want to do for your fortieth? Drinks? Dinner? A weekend away or perhaps a big party? Just say the word and we'll get organising it!'

Everyone else sitting around this lounge is in agreement that they will help contribute to whatever it is I wish to do to mark the occasion, and now all eyes are on me for the first time this evening. Before this, all the attention was either on my new house that I was showing everybody or on each other as they all chatted about their recent news. I'm the one in the spotlight, a position I used to enjoy being in but now not so much, because with secrets like mine, it's far better if I blend in to a crowd than be the focal point of it.

'Oh, erm. I don't know. I hadn't really thought about it,' I say, which is a half-truth. With so much going on recently, my birthday was hardly the top of my list of priorities. 'I think I just want a quiet one.'

That is the truth; I hardly want to be seen partying like a rock star on my fortieth birthday while the memory of my late husband's funeral is still fresh in everybody's minds. For obvious reasons, nobody in the room challenges me on what I've just said, totally understanding my desire for peace and quiet this year, so with my wishes stated, the conversation can move on.

When it does, I take a brief moment to watch the three

couples around me enjoying each other's company and, for a second, I think about telling them about Roger. I'm sure they'd be thrilled that I have a new man in my life because they'll just want me to be happy after Drew. They'll want to meet him and welcome him into this friendship group and find out his opinions on topics that they all love to discuss like politics, movies and where the best place to find some winter sun in January is. But I'm not ready for any of that yet and I dare say Roger isn't either.

We'll keep taking things slowly.

That seems to be working out well for us both so far.

At least I think it is...

EIGHT

GREG

It's not easy to write a letter while having to contend with the loud music from the flat directly above me or the loud cries from the revellers down on the busy city street below my apartment window, but I'm giving it my best.

It'll take a lot more than a noisy Friday night in Manchester to put me off my correspondence with Alice.

By my count, this will be the fifth letter I have written to HMP Carlisle and, in particular, to one of the newest inmates to reside on the wing kept specifically for those sentenced to the most serious of crimes. I wasn't sure if I would ever receive a response from Alice Richardson when I first wrote to her, telling her that I had seen her case in the news and believed she was innocent. First of all, I did not believe that I was the only red-blooded male in the country who had seen the photos of the attractive woman in the newspapers and decided to reach out in the hope they might get a bite back. But unlike any other guy who might have been writing to Alice since she went behind bars, I actually have substance in what I am saying, as I knew the man she is accused of killing.

So far, I have been careful in what I have revealed to Alice, only saying that I was a former friend of Drew and little more. I can't have her knowing I'm currently dating Fern, the woman I think put her in prison, in case she suspects I am Fern's ally. Alice is hardly likely to agree to meet me if she thinks I am just going to see her to laugh in her face and tell her that Fern is having a great time on the outside while she languishes on the inside, and that is my goal with the current letter I am composing.

To meet Alice.

If I can do that, I will tell her in person everything I am doing and how it could, hopefully, result in her being released.

I have no idea if Alice or indeed anybody in the prison authorities will accept my visitation request, but I have to try, just like I have to keep trying to negotiate Fern into a position where she might slip up and tell me what she did to Drew. If there is one trait that I can be defined by in my life then it is one of dogged determination. If I set my mind to something then I have to achieve it, no matter the odds or even if it's to my own detriment. I was like that in the police, which I'm sure is the reason why I burnt out and had to leave that line of work barely halfway through my career in the force. There's no doubt my aptitude for trying can result in exhaustion and sacrifice, but that's just the way I am wired, and especially when it comes to seeing justice is done.

Someone might wonder why I would bother getting myself so involved in the lives of Fern and Alice, but the way I see it why wouldn't I? If a person can lay their head down on their pillow at night and sleep easily knowing there is an injustice then good for them. But not me.

Alice deserves her freedom.

Fern deserves what is coming to her.

But it's not how much is at stake for Fern and Alice legally that is making my hands shake a little as I move my pen across this page. It's also what might be at stake for me and my personal life, too. As my relationship with Alice develops through this series of letters, I am becoming more fond of her by the day.

It was impossible to quench the thrill I felt when I got back to my apartment block one night, after a long and laborious day of salesmanship, to find there was an envelope inside my pigeonhole with a prison emblem stamped across it. I tore it open as quickly as I could, hoping it was Alice's first reply to me and not just some correspondence from a prison warden who was telling me to stop bothering their inmate. Thankfully, it was the response I'd been hoping for and, as my eyes flitted across the precise handwriting on the page before me, I felt my heart rate increasing, which told me this was already about more to me than just getting justice for a wronged individual.

The way Alice curled up her Ks and crossed her Ts on the page intrigued me almost as much as the content of the words she had so elegantly written, and I would be lying if I said the thought of her sitting at a desk with a pen and a piece of paper and giving me her full attention didn't make me smile. She thanked me for writing to her and believing in me and said that such letters of support were about the only things giving her the strength to keep going in her circumstances. But I also detected a sense of resignation in her words, as if she appreciated there were people out there who believed in her, but also accepted that such shows of support were hardly likely to make a difference in the grand scheme of things. I tried my best to dispel that notion in my letters that followed that first one by telling her I was an ex-policeman who felt there were ways her case could be reopened; but there is only so much I can do from so far away to improve her mood with just the strokes of a pen. I need to be with her, sitting right in front of her. Only then can I make her see that I could really be the one to change her fortunes, and I want to tell her exactly how I'll do that.

Beyond my increasing fondness for the damsel in distress,

this is about seeing Fern pay for what she did to my old tennis buddy, so I must remain focused on that goal. That is why I concentrate on finishing this latest letter before sealing it in an envelope and leaving my apartment to go down to the street to put it in the post box. With a bit of luck, Alice will receive it early next week, and when she is told she has a visiting request from me, she will, I hope, accept it.

Ignoring the drunken cheers of a group of students who live in one of the neighbouring apartment blocks, I'm on my way back into my own when I receive a text message. Checking my phone, I see it is from Fern, and when I read what she has sent me, I instantly know she has had a few drinks tonight. That's because the content of her message alongside the time of night suggests to me that this is what some people might term 'a booty call'.

Fern is drunk. Fern is lonely.

Fern wants company.

While I'm exhausted and was literally on my way back upstairs to get ready for bed after completing the only item on my to-do list this evening, I know I can't pass up an opportunity like this one. I'm not talking about sex. I'm talking about the fact that Fern is inebriated and, therefore, might be more inclined to say something to me that she might later regret.

Could this be the night when I get her to loosen her lips and say something about Drew and, more specifically, something about what she might have done to him that no one else alive knows about?

There's only one way to find out.

I quickly type out a message to Fern, replying to her suggestion that I come and visit her while she is lying in her bed all by herself.

Like the good boyfriend she thinks I am, I tell her that I'm on my way.

NINE

FERN

I know I shouldn't have drunk so much at my own housewarming party, and I know I'm probably going to regret inviting Roger to come and keep me company now that all my friends have left, but screw it. A woman has needs and as soon as my new man gets here, I am going to get to work on fulfilling some of those needs.

While Roger was very quick to accept my suggestive invitation for him to come and join me at this late hour on a Friday night, it is going to take a little more time for him to actually make his way across the city to be here with me. Until his arrival, I keep myself busy by topping my glass up with wine and swaying a little to the music still playing in the lounge.

This particular song was one that Drew and I danced to on many occasions over the last few years when we found ourselves on a night out, either just the two of us or with friends. But while I am missing a dance partner, I am not letting that ruin what for me was always a fun song and, to prove it, I make sure to turn up the music as I keep swaying my hips.

I'm well aware that my level of inebriation tonight means that I will be suffering from a dreaded hangover tomorrow, a thing that will likely only serve to increase any anxiety that lingers in my subconscious mind about Drew, Rory and what I did to them. I definitely could do without a day of wallowing in self-pity, and I most certainly could do without any nightmares, especially ones occurring in a mind affected by alcohol. But I'm too far past the point of doing anything to change the consequences for tomorrow, so I just embrace it and enjoy the benefits of my overindulgence this evening.

When I'm feeling this good, the last thing I care about is getting caught for my crimes.

After dancing to a couple more songs and finishing another glass of wine, I'm starting to worry that Roger might have changed his mind and decided not to come here tonight after all, leaving this to ultimately end as a party for one rather than two. Then I check my phone and see that I have a missed call and a message from him, and it's the message that tells me that he is outside and has been knocking on my front door for the last two minutes.

Oops. I guess I didn't hear him over the music.

Turning the volume down a little before skipping through the hallway to the door, I fling it open to find Roger looking far less energetic than I feel at this present moment. I have a feeling I know how to perk him up, so I reach out and grab the collar of his shirt before pulling him into my house and slamming the door shut behind him.

My lips are instantly on his and, while it takes him a few seconds to get on my wavelength, he soon matches my level of passion. Before he has even had time to wipe his feet on my new doormat and ask me how my evening has been, I am ripping off his shirt and dragging him into the lounge before pushing him down onto one of the sofas.

I quickly straddle him and keep my lips on his while removing my own top half of clothing and, if it wasn't clear what I had in mind for my man when he came here, he must certainly know what I have planned now. I get the sense that he might be slightly reluctant to be moving this fast, but I just put that down to him being a little shy and he soon finds his own rhythm to match mine.

Another song plays that used to remind me of Drew, but I am only thinking about the man I am with now and, after we have had quite wild, breathless sex, I tell Roger that for the first time in our relationship, I would like him to spend the entire night with me. He doesn't argue, not that I believe any man would after what I've just done to him, and I quickly turn off the music and the lights in the lounge before leading him upstairs for round two.

It's funny because I bet if I was a fly on the wall in the homes of any of my friends who came to my party tonight, I would hear them all talking sympathetically about me, and saying how it was such a shame that I was now alone and didn't want to do anything big for my birthday because of what I'd lost this year. If only they could see me now, running around my house with a very handsome and very naked man. They would be surprised, certainly, and I already can't wait for a few more months to pass when it will be a little more socially acceptable for me to tell them that I have moved on.

Then they won't be feeling sorry for me.

They'll be feeling envious.

It's only after Roger and I have done what we needed to do for a second time that we pause to draw breath. The pair of us lie beside each other on our backs, staring up at the ceiling with our hands resting on top of our naked torsos and a whole load of endorphins whizzing around our bodies. I'm quite happy to just exist in this state for as long as possible, but Roger seems intent on seizing this opportunity to become even more intimate with me.

I get that hint when he brings up Drew.

'Does it feel weird being with me and not him?' he asks me,

which sounds like a self-conscious question. Is my new man judging himself against my old one? If so, he has nothing to worry about there, and I prove that by laying my head on his chest and telling him how much better he is in the bedroom than the late doctor ever was. That might sound a little harsh on my ex-husband, but screw it, it's the truth, and I'm guessing it was what Roger was almost hoping to hear me say. But he's not quite done being a little needy yet.

'You must miss him,' he says quietly as I can hear the sound of his heartbeat in his chest returning to its normal rate after its rapid increase since he was pulled through my front door. 'I mean, don't get me wrong. I love that I'm with you now and am glad we're so good together. But you can be honest with me. Do you still find yourself thinking about him a lot?'

I realise then Roger is after a deeper conversation than I first realised, so I lift my head off his chest and look him in the eye. Then, because he is obviously being honest and a little vulnerable with me, I feel like I should try and be the same.

'Of course,' I say. 'He was my husband. I'll never forget about him, nor do I want to. But when I'm with you, it is all about you. I promise.'

Roger smiles at me before I give him a kiss, but it seems there's still something more.

'I guess what I'm getting at is, in my mind, Drew was this perfect guy that I'll probably never be able to compete with,' he goes on. 'He was a doctor. He cared for people, probably saved lives. Made good money. Gave you everything you ever wanted. No doubt introduced you to people that I could never get near. I'm just a salesman and a pretty poor one at that.'

'Don't put yourself down,' I say, unsure where this side of Roger has come from. He is opening up to me and that tells me this is progressing from just being about sex and a bit of fun to really going somewhere one day, which I don't think I would mind at all.

'You are great,' I go on, reaffirming how happy I am with him. 'I wouldn't be with you if you weren't.'

I do mean that last sentiment, because while on the face of it Roger is not quite as good a catch as Drew was, I think that's why I like being with him. Would I like it if Roger was a little more ambitious? Lived in a nicer part of the city? Could take me to a few social events that I'd never normally get access to? Sure, but they're not dealbreakers. After marrying and living with a lying cheat, at this stage of my life I'm happy to just take being with an honest man who cares about me.

I wink at Roger and hope that has done enough to ease any paranoia he might have about always being second to Drew. But has it worked?

'I appreciate that, but let's be honest. I am not quite on his level, am I?' he says. 'Do you know what might help? Hearing about some of his weaknesses. Mistakes he made. I think if I knew that he wasn't just this amazing guy who was taken away from you so suddenly then it might make me feel like I actually belong with you.'

I stare at Roger and really think about what he has just said. In his mind, he is second best to Drew, an option I went with only because my husband was found dead on a beach and, because of that, he feels inferior to the memory of him. That is not how I see it at all, and he should know that too.

'You know Drew was having an affair before he died,' I say. 'It was in the news. You know he wasn't perfect. Far from it.'

'Yeah, but that's just what the newspapers say. I want to hear about it from you.'

'About what?'

'About what happened between the two of you.'

'I only found out about them after his death,' I remind him, not drunk enough to forget to maintain that very important lie.

'There must have been signs before he died that he was up

to something though,' Roger goes on. 'You really had no idea he was having an affair until after he died?'

Now I'm frowning because I'm not sure why Roger is prying so much into what is obviously a very sensitive subject. He must recognise that I'm troubled, as he quickly tells me to forget about it and tries to kiss me. I'm not in the mood now and, to prove it, I get out of bed and put on my dressing gown.

'Hey, I'm sorry. I shouldn't have asked,' Roger says, trying to entice me back into bed, but the moment has long been lost now and, to confirm it, I tell him that he should join me in getting out of the bed too.

'I think you should stay at your place tonight,' I say, tying my dressing gown across my naked body. 'I've just remembered I've got to be up early tomorrow. Sorry.'

With that, what had been a wonderful evening is suddenly ruined.

TEN

GREG

It's been four days since I almost screwed up at Fern's place and completely ruined any chance I had of eliciting a confession from her about Drew's death. I say *almost* because, even though she told me to leave her house that night and didn't message me for several hours the following day, she has eventually become responsive to me and my affections again and, fortunately, we seem to be back on track.

I know I pushed things a little by prying and trying to get her to open up about Drew's faults, but it seemed like it was worth a try, particularly when Fern was so obviously drunk when I turned up at her house on Friday night. She proved just how low her inhibitions were when she dragged me into her home and practically pounced on me and, while I had little choice but to go along with what she wanted to do, I can't say my heart was in it quite as much as hers was. All I cared about was getting to the point where we were lying in that pleasant postcoital haze so I could see if her tongue might be loose enough to say something interesting about Drew, something the police don't know, or anybody else for that matter. But despite treading as carefully as I could, I must have spooked her because she shut down quickly and I lost my opportunity of hearing something that might have been useful. However, the main thing is that I am still close to Fern and, after she had finally messaged me the following day to apologise for abruptly telling me to leave, I apologised too for stirring up any deep-seated feelings she has about Drew. I told her in my message that it had not been my intention to upset her.

Fern seemed to buy that, as she said the problem was with her, not with me, and that she's finding it difficult to get over Drew and the lies he told her, which I made sure to tell her was perfectly understandable. Then I made sure to tell her that I was here for her to talk to about anything if she needed me to listen and, with that seemingly selfless statement made, I moved our messages back on to more light-hearted topics, ensuring things didn't get too heavy between us before Fern is ready for them to do so. But while Friday night was ultimately a failure, at least on my part, I have sewn a few seeds in Fern's mind and shown another side to me, which is important. I can't have her just thinking of me as a guy she can call when she is drunk and lonely. I need to be the guy she tells everything to one day.

And I do mean everything.

However, I have somebody else who is my priority today and, as I park my car and stare at the ominous walls of Carlisle prison, I am thinking more about Alice than Fern, because it is the prisoner I am here to see after she accepted my request for a visit.

Leaving my vehicle and trudging across the grey tarmac beneath a sky that is just as dull, I am nervous, although not because this will be my first time setting foot inside a prison.

I'm nervous because I am finally going to meet Alice in person.

After signing in and waiting patiently for the clock on the wall above the reception to show the precise time when visiting hours here begin, I am led along a brightly lit corridor by a warden in a black and white uniform towards a locked door. There is a jumble of keys on the ring that hangs from his belt and, as he finds the right one to slot into the lock, I look at the three other visitors who are standing here with me. They all look just as pensive as I feel, and I guess nobody enjoys having to come to a place like this. I wonder who they are. Husbands? Wives? Brothers? Mothers? Friends? All of them visiting a loved one on the inside to remind them that there is somebody out there waiting for their release. Their appearance here might be the only thing that keeps a person going, and, as we move through the door and enter the visiting room, I see those people before me.

There's a woman with very short hair sitting at the table nearest to me and her face lights up when she sees the woman to my left. Behind her is a younger female who looks pale and tired but who also livens up when she sees that she has company. The table to her left has an overweight inmate sitting at it and, at first, she doesn't seem that fussed that she has a visitor, but she eventually smiles too as she sits back in her seat and prepares to welcome in her loved one.

Then I see who is at the table at the back of the room.

I feel my pulse quicken slightly as I lay eyes on Alice, and when I see her looking at me it only seems to get faster. As I walk over to her table, it becomes obvious that I am the one she has been writing to all this time and I see her shift a little nervously in her seat as I approach. But I don't want her to be apprehensive, so I try to disarm her with a big smile and, when I reach my chair, I ask her if it's okay for me to sit down before I do so.

As I settle into the uncomfortable plastic chair upon which I will stay for the duration of this 'meeting', I regard the woman across the table from me. Now that I am closer to her, I can see some of the effects that being in here have had on her since her sentencing. Her blonde hair is not as well-groomed as it was in the photos I saw in the papers, but her green eyes are just as vivid and captivating as in the media images, and it is with those eyes that she is doing her own silent appraisal of me and my appearance.

I wonder if she likes what she sees. I've made the effort to present well to her, making sure I was clean-shaven, and wearing smart clothes. There's only so much a guy can do to really make his appearance dazzle, but I'm confident my classic good looks should be enough for her to at least find me handsome enough to be intrigued. It sure seemed to work with Fern. Then again, Alice most likely couldn't care less about my looks. What I have to say can affect her, though, so I break the silence between us.

'Thank you for allowing me to see you,' I say, placing my hands on the table to try and appear as relaxed as I can, even if I don't feel that way on the inside. 'And thank you for replying to my letters.'

'What do you want?' Alice asks me, wasting no time with pleasantries, but I suppose a woman in her position has little use for being polite, as it'll take a lot more than a few 'pleases' and 'thank yous' to get her out of here.

'Like I said in my letters, I believe you are innocent, and I want to help you get out of prison.'

'How can you do that?'

Alice already looks like she is thinking this is just going to be one big waste of time. But I'm ready to show her that I am deadly serious.

'By proving that it was Fern who killed Drew and not you.'

That's certainly got the prisoner's attention and, after she has glanced at the warden standing with his back to the wall to our left, she leans in a little closer to the table.

'What the hell are you talking about?'

'I believe that it was Fern who killed Drew, or at least she planned to. I think that she was helped by Rory and that will explain why he died too shortly afterwards.'

To my surprise, Alice looks stunned by what I have just said.

'Wait, you don't suspect Fern yourself?' I ask her.

'No! I thought it was Rory who killed Drew and framed me and then he killed himself to deal with the guilt.'

That's an interesting theory Alice has there, but mine is better.

I believe mine is the truth and, confident now that Alice is warmed up to me, at least to the point where she is open to what I really came here to tell her, I launch into it.

I enlighten Alice as to why I am so convinced Fern is the real guilty party, running through everything from how I am an old friend of Drew's and how he mentioned to me about Fern's jealous tendencies, to how I am convinced Fern found out about her husband's affair much sooner than she let on to the police. I also refer to my past as a policeman because that has to be relevant and will qualify me a little more as the best person to help in a situation like this one. But it's what I say after all that which really makes Alice's eyes go wide. While everything I have said so far has been surprising to her, my latest admission blows her mind.

'I am currently in a relationship with Fern,' I tell her.

'What?'

Alice looks mortified, as if I've just said the last thing in the world she thought I was going to say.

'Don't worry. It's not real, at least not for me anyway,' I tell her quickly. 'I'm just trying to get as close to her as I can so I can try and catch her out.'

I was expecting that my announcement of my closeness to Fern would give Alice hope that I might be able to uncover the truth, but my revelation only seems to have troubled her.

'What are you doing? What kind of sick game is this?' she

asks me as she moves back away from the table, and it surprises me how much I hate seeing her increase the distance between us.

'Game? I'm not playing a game. I'm trying to help you.'

'Help me? You've just told me Fern is the one who framed me and then you said you're dating her. What is this? Are you here to torment me?'

Alice looks like she is ready to stand up and leave this room and, when I see her glance again at the warden, I fear she is just about to tell him that she would like to go. Before she can do that, I lean over the table and, even though I know the warden who brought me in here told me not to get too close to the prisoners, I have to make my point very clear to Alice.

'I am on your side. I am doing this for you. Trust me, I am going to get you out of here. I promise.'

While the nearest warden to us is quickly over to give me a warning about getting too close, I am pleased to see that Alice seems to have taken my stern statement on board, and she looks more likely to stay where she is, for the time being anyway. Once the warden has gone, I back it up.

'I came here because I wanted to tell you that I am working on Fern and hope to have a breakthrough there soon,' I say. 'This is about the right thing being done. I want justice, for you and for Drew. In the meantime, is there anything you can think of that might help me? Anything at all.'

Alice thinks about it for a moment before she answers.

'You need to talk to Detective Tomlin. Tell him what you've told me. He's never suspected Fern, probably because I haven't either. If you tell him what you think, he might question her again.'

'I am going to go and see him while I am in Carlisle,' I confirm. 'But I have to tread carefully. I can't risk him tipping off Fern about who I am and what I am doing.'

'I understand,' Alice says, and it feels good to see that she is trusting me again. It feels even better when I hear what she has to say next.

'Please be careful,' she says, getting her message across before our visit is up. 'If you are right and it was that bitch who put me in here then you have to watch your back. She's dangerous.'

I promise Alice I can handle Fern, while simultaneously feeling a little giddy that she cares about what happens to me. Or maybe she just wants to make sure that her last hope at getting out of here doesn't end up in prison too.

Or worse.

End up dead like Drew and Rory.

ELEVEN

FERN

I'm not sure there is a single person who enjoys visiting a graveyard. Not only are they instant reminders of one's mortality but they are generally not very fun places to be. They're quiet, sombre environments, sometimes not very well maintained and, on a bad weather day like this one is today, downright depressing.

I can hear the sound of raindrops bouncing off the top of my umbrella as I make my way along the path that cuts through this graveyard that is Drew's final resting place. It was a joint decision between myself and Drew's parents to have him buried here. The grounds belong to St Meridian's Church and it's a building that played a significant role in the late doctor's life.

Drew was christened here when he was a baby; he attended services here every Sunday as he was going through school; and, even though he had drifted away from religion somewhat in his adult years, he still had enough of a connection to these grounds for it to be a suitable final resting place.

As I glance at the spire to my left that rises up above dozens of gravestones protruding from the tufty grass beside the wet path, I am instantly transported back to my wedding day. I can vividly recall arriving at this church with my father, Tony, as all the other guests waited inside for the ceremony to begin. Unlike today, the sky was blue and the air was warm as I stepped out of the car and linked arms with Dad before we made our grand entrance into the church and all eyes were on me as I moved down the aisle, my white dress flowing behind me.

I'd originally been unsure about marrying in a church and had considered a more modern venue, but it was Drew, or rather his parents, who gently persuaded me to marry at this site, and on the day I was glad they had done that. Such an historic venue, with the sunlight streaming through the stained-glass windows and not a spare seat to be had in the packed pews, contributed to the sense of occasion I felt as I reached the altar and took my place beside the groom. As we said our vows in the eyes of God and made our way back out of the church as husband and wife, a large organ was played perfectly, the music becoming the soundtrack to our very first steps into marriage.

The church doesn't look quite so special on a cloudy day like this one, nor can I say it holds many good memories for me any more. While Drew appeared to be holier than thou while he was standing beside me and reciting his vows, he soon proved that he was not beyond sin, and if there is a heaven and a hell, as Drew's parents keenly believe there is, I have a feeling I know which place the late doctor has ended up in.

Then again, I expect I'll be joining him when I depart this life too one day.

Pushing that unsettling thought from my mind, I forge on through the rain until I reach the gravestone I have come here to visit. Then I stare at the inscription for several long minutes.

DREW DEVLIN

I tend to just look at that part of the headstone and little else because, to me, it's the only part that is truthful. The line underneath it that says **Beloved Husband** is certainly a lie, right up there with many of the lies Drew told me himself when he was still around to do such things. Unfortunately, it had to be inscribed on the headstone to allow me to keep up appearances as the grieving widow who wished her husband was still alive, and that's also the reason I am here today. **Doting Son** also went on there, as did **Respected Doctor**. Knowing my late husband, he would have wanted the word *Doctor* before his name, in much larger lettering, because that was the type of guy he was; he loved his job title or, rather, he loved the impact it had on people when they found out what he did for a living. But I've made sure his profession has been buried a little further down on the headstone, there just to satisfy his family but not prominent enough to be obvious to any passers-by. I don't want people taking second glances at this grave or thinking the person buried here is any more respectable or smarter than anybody else buried here, because the truth is he's not. Drew might have thought he was better than everybody else but, just like everybody else, there's not much left in the end but a pile of bones and a few memories.

I make the effort to visit Drew's grave once a week, delivering a bouquet of fresh flowers and staring pensively at his burial site for as long as I can be bothered to because, that way, it looks like I miss him and that reduces the chances of anybody suspecting that I was the one who actually helped put him in this place. Fulfilling my role as the grieving wife, I kneel slightly and place the latest bunch of flowers on the grass by my feet before taking a step back and having another quiet moment. If anybody could see me now, they would surely just think of me as yet another heartbroken person who was mourning a lost loved one, which is the idea. Unfortunately, there is nobody around at this time to see my 'performance' because the rain has seen to that. I'm the only one who has braved the elements to come here today, but it had to be that way. I'm getting my hair and nails done tomorrow and going shopping for some new furniture for my lounge the day after, so this is the only time I could fit in a visit. However, the fact that nobody else is around allows me an opportunity to say a few things out loud here, things that no one else can hear except me and possibly Drew's spirit, so I get right to it.

'You might think that you're clever, coming to me in my dreams as you have been doing,' I say, the fatigue from yet another bad night's sleep still creeping at the edges of my mind. 'But I know the nightmares will become less as I start to forget about you, just like everybody else will forget about you eventually too.'

I wasn't sure about talking out loud to an inanimate object but, now that I've started conversing with Drew's headstone, it actually feels quite good, particularly as I am trying to banish his memory by doing so.

'However I feel in my dreams is not how I feel when I am awake,' I go on, warming to my theme. 'I don't regret what I did because you deserved it. You brought this on yourself. You and *her*. Things could have been so different. I'm turning forty soon, and you could have been there beside me to help me celebrate. As it is, you made your choices and you suffered the consequences.'

I stop short of telling Drew's spirit that he made his bed and now he has to lie in it, or, rather, he made his own grave and now he has to lie in it, which amuses me a little. But the thought of my impending birthday causes me to stop thinking about the man buried six feet beneath me and more about my own situation. With such a milestone in my life on the horizon, I have been spending more and more time thinking less about things I have done and more about things I haven't done.

One of those things is to have a baby.

The more time I have spent pondering the absence of a son or daughter in my life, the more I have realised it is something that I wanted more than I had first realised. With that rather startling realisation coming to me quite late in my life, at least in terms of my biological clock anyway, it means I don't have very long to take any action to change my circumstances.

If I want a baby, which I think I do, I'm going to have to start trying as soon as possible.

As it stands, Roger is the only suitable male candidate in my life who could give me what I am after. We are close and getting closer by the day, so what if I was to mention my broodiness to him? Would he tell me that he feels the same way and wishes us to try? Or would he freak out and run away, further reducing my chances of getting what I want?

I'm not sure but I do know one thing: there are no answers waiting for me here in this graveyard. This is the land for those who have already had their chance and, in the case of people like Drew, they blew it. I'm determined not to do that. We're only here once and we owe it to ourselves to chase down everything we want before it's too late.

As I turn and walk away from my late husband's grave with the rain still pitter-patting against my umbrella, I am fully determined to achieve my goals.

Little did I know it, but I wasn't the only one...

TWELVE

GREG

I consider my first visit with Alice a success, but there's one more person I have to see in Carlisle before I can head back to Manchester, and that is the man currently walking through this car park on his way into the police station.

'Detective Tomlin?'

I already know this is definitely the person who was in charge of Drew's murder investigation, because I have seen his photo in the news articles online, but I am being polite as I interrupt his movements.

'Yes?' he says, pausing and looking me up and down, as if he is instantly sizing me up and trying to ascertain whether I am a good guy or one of the many bad guys he comes across in his line of work.

'Hi, my name is Greg, and I was wondering if I could have a little bit of your time to talk about something important. It relates to one of your previous cases.'

'Which case?'

'Drew Devlin. But it also involves Rory Richardson and his death too.'

'Arberness?'

'That's right,' I say, confirming the detective's reference to that sleepy village several miles west of here that inexplicably saw its crime rate increase dramatically when Fern Devlin made it her home for a short while. Funnily enough, the crime rate there has returned to almost zero since she has left, and there certainly haven't been any more dead bodies reported since she went back to Manchester.

'What about it?' Tomlin asks me, clearly not willing to give me much time unless I can demonstrate I have something of significance to say to him. But it's complicated so I can't go through it all in just a few seconds, nor would I want to do it out here where anyone could hear us.

'There's a pub around the corner from here. Can I buy you a pint?' I ask Tomlin, and while the detective feigns being busy and not having much time to spare, I notice the glint in his eyes when I suggest a trip to the pub. As I know all too well from my own past in the police force, some of the best crime-solving work in this country is done in a quiet corner of a pokey pub over a couple of pints. Or at least that is what a detective or police officer will say when they try to justify exactly why they spent time drinking beer rather than pushing papers at their desk. 'Gathering intel' is the popular phrase often used, which sounds a lot better than 'needing a break from a stuffy station'; and after persuading Tomlin that I have something important to tell him, he agrees to come to the pub with me.

As we make the short walk there, I get the sense that this is a man who is feeling as worn down with police work as I was just before I made the decision to resign from the force and try my hand at being a salesman. I can tell that because of several things about his appearance and the way he moves. His scruffy suit that is a couple of sizes too big for him suggests that he is making little effort with his appearance, just as the uncombed hair and two-day stubble on the bottom half of his face points to it as well. He looks tired, though that is a given in his line of work, and the way his black shoes scuff across the bottom of the road as we cross the street also hints at a weariness to his character.

I sympathise with him, which is why, when we reach the pub, I make sure to pay for the two beers we order as well as the packet of crisps I offer him, and only when he is comfortably seated at a small table in the otherwise empty venue do I begin.

'I was once good friends with Drew,' I tell the detective, and that nugget of information seems to be enough for him to allow me to go on as he picks up his pint and takes his first sip. As he licks a little bit of the froth off his top lip, I remain focused on him rather than my own drink, because it is important that I do enough to convince this man that what I am about to tell him is the truth.

'We played tennis together back in Manchester, before he moved to Arberness. I never met his wife, Fern, but he talked about her from time to time, and while most of it was pretty benign stuff, there was one thing he said that stuck in my mind.'

'And that was?' Tomlin asks me as he tears open the bag of crisps.

'She got very jealous one evening when she found out he was messaging an old university friend. A female friend.'

'And? She sounds just like my ex-wife.'

Hmm, another cop with a failed marriage. I can't say I'm shocked.

'Yes, but in your marriage, jealousy just led to a divorce,' I say. 'In Fern's, the husband ended up dead.'

Tomlin stops chomping on the crisps and gives me his full attention.

'What are you getting at, Greg?'

'I believe that Fern found out about Drew's affair before his death, not after it like she made out to you and the rest of your colleagues.'

'And if she did?'

'Well, it's obvious, isn't it? She either killed him or plotted with Rory, Alice's partner, to have him killed.'

It's clearly not obvious to the detective; he just scoffs at my suggestion.

'And what evidence do you have to prove that?'

'Well, I'm working on that.'

'Ahh, you're working on it. That's reassuring. And how are you doing that?'

'By posing as Fern's new boyfriend and getting close enough to her to find out the truth.'

Tomlin doesn't scoff this time. He now looks deadly serious.

'You're posing as her boyfriend?'

'That's right. She doesn't know who I really am, which has allowed me to get close to her.'

'Is the relationship physical?'

'Reluctantly, yes. I've had no choice if I was to keep up the illusion.'

Tomlin still looks serious, and I know why, which is why I pre-empt what he is likely to say next.

'Look, I'm aware it's a crime to have sexual contact with a person while pretending to be someone else, but in this case, I think I'm justified. Fern is a killer and Alice has been framed. I'm convinced of it.'

'That doesn't give you the right to do what you're doing and you know it. You're taking an incredible risk by breaking the law to chase down this wild theory of yours. I'm going to pretend I didn't just hear about it, but I think you should reconsider your course of action.'

'Hear me out. Think about it. I know you and your colleagues think Alice killed Drew and that Rory, after one too many drinks, was feeling depressed about it all and drowned himself in a hot bathtub, but let's presume for a moment that such a story is just a little too neat and tidy. In your version, all the bows are wrapped up and everybody is taken care of, especially Fern, the wife of the cheating doctor.'

'Alice did it. There was evidence.'

'You mean the message sent to Drew from her phone telling him to meet her on the beach that night, as well as the murder weapon with her fingerprints on it? Just because that message came from Alice's phone, it doesn't mean that she sent it. Rory could have done that while she was in the shower and he could have been told to do it by Fern. And as for the spade that was used to strike Drew over the head with, it was one of the garden tools in Alice and Rory's garage. Of course it had her fingerprints on it. It's because she used it whenever she was gardening!'

Tomlin hears what I have to say before shaking his head.

'There was a thorough investigation and, based on all the evidence we presented to the courts, Alice was found guilty.'

'Because that was how Fern wanted it to look.'

Tomlin stares at me but he's no longer laughing, nor is he picking up his pint or reaching for another crisp.

'Look, I get it,' I say. 'No detective wants to be known as the guy who got it wrong. You have a reputation to uphold and you and your colleagues don't want to think that hours of your time have been wasted in the past and you have to reopen a case you already thought was closed. I appreciate that. Like I said, I was in the police force once and I know how much pressure there is to make arrests and get charges to stick.'

'But you're not a police officer any more, right? And you weren't a detective, I'm guessing? So how about you leave the crime solving to those of us qualified to do it?'

I bite my tongue at Tomlin's patronising remark and forge on.

'You've only seen the side of Fern that she has allowed you to see,' I say, my own pint sitting untouched before me – but I didn't come here to drink. 'There is another side to her, and I know about it because I was one of the few people, perhaps the only person, who Drew told. She got very jealous very quickly and was prone to overreacting if she thought her husband was up to something with another woman.'

'Many women would do the same. Doesn't mean she is a killer.'

'But how many men end up murdered on a beach, especially in a place like Arberness? It's very rare, isn't it? But that's what happened to Drew. While we know he was seeing another woman before he died, the question is, if Fern did find out about it, could that have been her revenge?'

'You don't think we thought of that?' Tomlin says with a shrug. 'The partner of the deceased is often the first suspect in cases like these. But we questioned Fern and were satisfied with her answers. More so, we found the evidence all pointed to one person and it was not her.'

'Yes, I know, it all pointed to Alice. But can't you see how Fern would have wanted it to look that way? She was her husband's mistress. The other woman. Fern's love rival. Imagine if she concocted a way to somehow get Alice to take the fall for a crime she didn't commit. Doesn't that sound like delicious revenge to you?'

'Only if Fern knew about the affair beforehand and she is adamant she did not. Besides, even if she did, it's still a very big step to arranging her husband's murder and framing an innocent woman. She could have just divorced him.'

'Didn't you listen to what I told you? She has a jealous streak and it was enough to worry Drew to the point where he mentioned it to me that night we spoke after tennis.'

Tomlin shakes his head and picks up his drink again, looking around the drab venue we are sitting inside as he does, a venue he has probably had more than his fair share of drinks in during his time in Carlisle.

'Why are you here?' he asks me. 'What do you hope to achieve with this?'

'I want to get justice for my late friend and also for Alice. I want to see Fern pay for what she did.'

'Then if you are right about this, you'll need evidence. What have you got?'

'Nothing. Fern has covered her tracks well.'

'That's convenient.'

'I will get something on her. If I could get a recorded confession would that be enough for you to charge her and release Alice?'

'A confession? Well of course, but let's just say she did do it, which I don't believe she did. Why on earth would she confess after she has already got away with it?'

'Because she trusts me,' I say, and only now do I feel confident enough to pick up my drink. 'She trusts me more and more every day.'

The next ten minutes are spent telling the detective that he just has to humour me enough to be willing to accept whatever evidence I am eventually able to deliver to him. That way, I'll know for sure that all my efforts with Fern won't be in vain. But there is another reason I am telling him my plan, and it is an even more serious one than trying to free an innocent woman from prison.

'If something bad happens to me, anything at all, it means Fern found out what I was looking into and she has got rid of me,' I say solemnly, well aware that I am risking my life by getting so close to a woman I believe to be dangerous.

Tomlin seems to think I am being a little dramatic there, but it is imperative that he takes what I have just told him onboard, and I do not allow the conversation to be over until he has promised me that if he hears of my demise, he will not let the trail run cold where I left it. He is to pick up my investigation himself and see it through, because anything happening to me only makes it more likely that Fern is the killer I think she is.

'I have to ask you something,' Tomlin says after a heavy moment. 'If you're really in as much danger as you believe you are, why are you doing this? Why are you risking your life for a friend who is already dead and a woman you barely know?'

It's a good question and while I offer what seems like a good answer, espousing my desire for justice to be served and the truth to come out, I make sure to stay quiet about the part where I am enamoured with Alice and harbour a desire for her to perhaps fall into my arms if and when she is a free woman again one day. I don't want Tomlin thinking I'm just saying and doing all of this out of some misguided sense of lust or even love for Alice, which is why I don't let him in on how I'm truly feeling about the innocent prisoner.

But which is it, lust or love?

One? The other? Both? I don't know. All I do know is I can't stop thinking about Alice, and not just because of her connection to Fern and Drew.

With our talk concluded, Tomlin tells me he has to get back to the station, so I follow him out of the pub and thank him for his time. Just before we separate, I ask him if I can have his phone number just in case I need to get in touch with him about anything I have discussed. He reluctantly gives me it. Then he departs and, as I watch the weary detective trudging back to his workplace, I wonder if has believed a word I have said.

It doesn't matter.

He'll believe me soon enough.

He'll believe me when I get that confession from Fern, and, as I take my phone out of my pocket, I have a feeling I know exactly when I am going to get it.

THIRTEEN

FERN

The decorating in my new home is progressing but the smell of fresh paint was giving me a headache. That's why I messaged Roger and asked him if we could do dinner at his place tonight instead of at mine. It's probably for the best because I'm long overdue seeing where he lives, and while he's already told me his home is nowhere near as decadent as mine, I'm game for a change of scene. But when Roger replied to my suggestion, he had one of his own. He told me that rather than eat at his place this evening, he would reserve us a table at a fancy Italian restaurant in the city centre. I couldn't argue with that and, with my mind full of delicious daydreams about doughballs, breadsticks and pasta, I told him to let me know when and where he wanted me to be and I would see him there.

The venue for our dinner date this evening turned out to be Boncelli's, a cosy little eatery with wood-fired ovens and plenty of photos of famous Italian landmarks hanging on the walls. It's one of those photos I am looking at now as Roger checks the wine menu in front of me. I'm enjoying looking at the image of the Colosseum in Rome and not just because it's an excellent piece of photography. It's because it has been a long time since I left the country and visited foreign shores. Maybe it is time to take a little trip and use some of the money I got from Drew's life insurance to pay for a city break or perhaps a week or two on a sun-kissed beach. That would be nice and I think about suggesting such a trip to Roger at some point during our meal tonight. Surely that will be an easy topic to discuss. But there is another topic that I am far more apprehensive about broaching with him.

It's the topic of trying for a baby before it's too late for me.

I decide to give Roger the chance to order his food and savour a little of his red wine before I spring the subject of kids on him, but it is not far from my mind as the evening progresses, and I continue to enjoy my time in his company. I'm reluctant to say this reminds me of the early days of mine and Drew's courtship, if only because of what ended up happening later in that relationship, but there are definitely some similarities.

Fancy restaurants. Easy conversation. Lingering looks. Humour. Comfort.

Dare I say, *love?*

Despite doing my best to take things slowly with Roger, I do feel I'm falling for him. He has many of the same qualities as Drew had, from his sense of humour to his educated mind, and then there are his good looks, which aren't crucial to the cause but hardly hurt. While there are some differences between the two men, namely Drew having a much more prestigious job than Roger has, not to mention my late husband had a far nicer home when I first met him than the one Roger currently resides in, there is one big difference that makes Roger the clear winner between them when all things are considered.

Unlike Drew, Roger has no secrets.

To me, that is the most important thing of all.

We're halfway through our main course, and a couple of

minutes into the latest operatic song softly coming from the sound system in here, when Roger tells me he has an early birthday present for me.

'I know you said you didn't want to make a fuss for your fortieth,' he starts with, recalling a conversation we had last week in which I told him I was just planning on having a quiet birthday as my next milestone rapidly approaches. It's only a week until I exit my thirties and you best believe I'm going to savour every single second until that day arrives. 'And I appreciate that because of what's happened recently. But I was thinking, how about the two of us do something? It can still be quiet, and I won't make a big fuss, but I think it would be a shame to let such a milestone pass without doing something to mark it.'

'What do you have in mind?' I ask him, my left hand wrapped around the stem of my wine glass and my eyes firmly on the dashing man in the smart black shirt sitting across the table from me.

'How about a night in a hotel?'

'Is this a present for me or for you?' I tease, and Roger laughs before telling me that it can be something we can both enjoy.

I don't need much persuading so I agree to his suggestion, and he tells me he will organise it all. The only thing I have to do is keep myself free that night, which won't be a problem because I'd already told my closest friends that I didn't want to do anything, and I imagine I'll be seeing my parents earlier in the day, leaving the evening open to do as I please.

It's yet another romantic gesture from the man I am becoming more enamoured with by the day and, just before we pick up our knives and forks again and resume our meals, I wonder if this might be the best time I'm going to get to say what I wanted to say tonight.

'Now please don't take this the wrong way because I'm

merely just thinking out loud here,' I begin tentatively. 'But with me turning forty, it's got me thinking a little bit about the future and some of the things I haven't done yet.'

'Things on your bucket list?' Roger asks me as he catches the waiter's eye to indicate that he'd like another bottle of wine when he gets a moment.

'Kind of. Not exactly. It's bigger than travelling or anything like that.'

'Oh, okay, what is it?'

As I thought, this is quite hard to just blurt out, and I am seriously considering not saying anything because I don't want to ruin this romantic meal by causing Roger to freak out and run from the restaurant. But the clock is ticking in more ways than one, so I take a deep breath and then just go for it.

'I've been thinking about a baby,' I say as I brace myself for Roger's reaction. Thankfully, it's nowhere near as bad as I feared it might be.

'Okay. A specific baby or just babies in general?' he quips, and I can't help but smile.

'Babies in general. Or rather, a baby I might have one day.'

'I see.'

Roger does look a little uncomfortable now, but this is always a tricky conversation for any new couple to have, so I remind myself of that before I push on.

'I'm not saying I want to get pregnant right away or anything like that. It's just that if I do want a baby then it's something I have to consider very soon.'

'I see,' Roger says, and if his nerves are jangling on the inside, he is doing a very good job of staying composed on the outside.

'I honestly thought I was fine to not have kids,' I go on. 'But all the talk of my fortieth recently has got me thinking and now I'm not so sure. I just don't want any regrets, I suppose.'

'That's understandable.'

'Have you ever thought about kids?'

'Me?' Roger shifts in his seat a little and looks around for the waiter, but he's not here to interrupt us yet so he has to answer the question.

'I mean, it's not something I'm opposed to if that's what you're asking. I guess I've just not thought about it too much.'

'You're lucky. Us women don't get as long as you men to make our minds up about such a thing.'

'That is true. Then again, you women don't have to memorise dozens of football scores every weekend to recite to your mates down the pub later that night.'

'Hey, I'll have you know I can remember a set of football scores just as well as any man,' I say, and while I know we're only joking and riffing off male and female stereotypes, this is still a serious thing to be discussing and, thankfully, Roger acknowledges it once the joking is over.

'If what you are asking me is would I be interested in perhaps having a baby with you one day then the answer is yes, it's something I would happily consider when the time is right,' he tells me, and I feel like a weight has been lifted off my shoulders. His answer means that I am not wasting my time with him and, because of that, I can relax a little and not feel so rushed.

Then again, I still don't have forever.

But that's enough serious stuff for one evening, and, as the waiter arrives at our table with that second bottle of wine Roger ordered, I am willing to move on to another subject. Something less heavy. Something simple. The baby stuff can be put on the backburner again.

For tonight, at least.

But once a woman like me has something on her mind, it's not easily forgotten about and that is why, as our delicious meal progresses, all I am thinking about now is the precise moment I will fully commit to trying to start a family.

I just don't mention it again to Roger for the rest of the night.

I'll let him enjoy his wine while I enjoy thoughts of the two of us one day becoming three.

FOURTEEN

GREG

While I was confident my deception of Fern was going well, I could never be one hundred per cent sure that I had her under my spell, as there was always room for a few doubts to creep in. But those doubts have been well and truly dismissed tonight after Fern essentially told me she was thinking about trying for a baby one day before asking me if I was on the same page as her.

I had to pretend that I was and so made sure to tell her what she wanted to hear, which was that yes, I could see myself being a dad one day and was open to the idea of a child. However, I can't think of anything worse than starting a family with a woman like Fern, and that is why I need to make sure I have successfully achieved my aim of bringing her down well before she officially has us both trying for a baby. If the stakes weren't high enough already, they have increased now. If I don't get what I need soon and have to start delaying Fern's baby wishes, she may choose to leave me and then I'll never get another chance to elicit the truth from her.

Fortunately, I have already been making progress on my plan and believe that I have the perfect occasion in which I stand the best chance of getting Fern to slip up and say something self-incriminating that I can secretly record on my phone. It's her fortieth next week and, after my suggestion at dinner tonight, she is keeping that night free. She thinks I am taking her away for a quiet night in a hotel. I am taking her to a hotel all right, but it will be anything but quiet.

That's because I have been diligently working away in the background to set up what is going to be quite the surprise party for Fern.

I suspect the word surprise will be an understatement.

After my meeting in the pub with Detective Tomlin the other day, I messaged one of Fern's best friends, Claire, via social media. I was able to establish that she was close to Fern as Claire featured a lot in many of Fern's older online posts. Once I'd established a connection between the pair, I did a little snooping around on Claire's social media account and saw her most recent post from last weekend, in which she had taken a photo in Fern's new house with the caption: *'Housewarming party at my bestie's new place!'* That told me all I needed to know about these two women still being close, so with that I reached out to Claire via a private message.

I'd set up a fake account on Instagram under my alias of Roger just before I 'met' Fern, and have followed numerous other accounts in the hopes that many of them would simply be polite enough to follow me back. That is how it turned out and that is how my fake profile shows that I have over two hundred followers, giving it social legitimacy. It wouldn't have looked good to have zero followers. Fern might have thought I was either a loner, or worse correctly figured it was a fake account, but thanks to the 'follow me and I'll follow you' unwritten rule of social media, I have built quite the database of 'friends', which is more than enough to throw Fern, and indeed Claire, off the scent when it comes to my Instagram account.

After messaging Claire, I apologised for introducing myself

to her in such an unsociable way but explained that it was simply the only way I could reach out to her as Fern hadn't introduced us in person yet. I explained that I was dating Fern and expressed how vital it was that Claire didn't corroborate this story with her best friend just yet, as Fern wanted to keep her new relationship private after what happened with Drew, which was surely understandable. I finished my message to Claire by saying that the reason for contacting her was that I felt it would be a shame if Fern's fortieth birthday passed without a party and, even though she was far too self-conscious after Drew's death to organise one for herself, we should pick up the mantle for her and arrange it ourselves. But crucially, it had to be a surprise.

I had been extremely nervous as I waited to hear back from Claire; I had no idea whether she would trust what I was saying or message Fern to tell her that some weirdo had just reached out to her claiming to be her new boyfriend. Fortunately, Claire seemed to understand my request for privacy and, instead of being suspicious, she was simply overjoyed at the news that her best friend had already started to move on from Drew and had found a little happiness after such a tough time lately.

Claire asked me what I had in mind in terms of the party for Fern, and I told her that I could book one of the function rooms in the hotel I had earmarked as the place I was going to take her for our 'quiet night'. Claire told me that she thought my plan was a great one, and after she accepted the responsibility of messaging around the rest of her family and friends and telling them where to be and when, she ended her message by saying she couldn't wait to meet me and she couldn't believe her best friend had been keeping a secret from her for all this time.

While it was tempting to reply to Claire and say that Fern was a master of keeping secrets and there were far more things about her that she was yet to learn, I was sensible and stayed in character long enough to say I was looking forward to the party too and would see her soon. With that, the party was set, and I've been receiving the occasional message from Claire ever since, with updates about how many people she has had a positive response back from after she invited them to the short-notice event. So far, there are almost thirty people going, which is a good number, not that the number of attendees is of great concern to me. The only thing I am interested in is making sure Fern has a brilliant time, and by that I mean drinks so much that when we fall into bed at the end of the night and I initiate another deep conversation about Drew, she'll be far too drunk to stop herself telling me everything. Then again, the more people that come, the more likely she is to party, so hopefully Claire's updates over the next few days will tell me that the guest list is growing.

The more, the merrier.

And I really want to get Fern merry.

The way I see it, Fern's fortieth might be my one and only chance to get Fern to a place mentally where she can tell me what she did to Drew without risking leaving it any longer and our relationship ending. It's now or never and, to increase the odds in my favour, I have adapted my plan. I am going to share a secret with Fern after the party, something fictional and something designed to make her feel like getting something off her chest as well. It's worth a shot and, speaking of shots, I hope Fern's friends at the party buy her plenty of those to aid my cause even further.

With my plan for Fern firmly in motion, my thoughts drift to Alice as I return once again to my feeble apartment, an apartment where Fern suggested she could visit me tonight before I turned her down and booked the restaurant instead. It was either that or take down the wallchart I have up and I couldn't be bothered to do that. As I think about Alice, I feel a little guilty for enjoying a nice evening in a fancy restaurant, having waiters running around after me, while she is languishing in a place where service is non-existent, as are good food and drink. Life is unfair, but I intend to show her soon enough that it is not all bad. In the meantime, I just have to hope that Alice can stay safe in what is a very dangerous environment. The last thing I want is for her to come to any harm before I can save her.

But just like everything else going on at the moment, the clock is ticking there too.

FIFTEEN

ALICE

For a woman in my position, it's strange to ever think that something could be too good to be true. But that's what I've been thinking for the last few days as, recently, the one woman in this prison who has been tormenting me ever since I arrived here has decided to leave me alone.

I have no idea why Kelly, the biggest bully in this place, has not even so much as looked at me during mealtimes or leisure time on the wing, not that I'm complaining. It's just strange considering how much fun she seemed to be having teasing me about being in here when I first arrived, not to mention the few occasions she threatened to get physical with me.

'I guess she got bored and moved on to somebody else,' Siobhan, my only friend in here, said to me when I mentioned it to her yesterday. 'It's like that in prison. Don't try to predict things. The only thing you can count on in here is the door to your cell being locked every night. Other than that, all bets are off.'

While it wasn't exactly comforting to hear my friend describe prison life as essentially just one big unpredictable puzzle that is impossible to solve, it was at least good to know that Kelly ignoring me was not unusual. That allows me to relax a little more and, while I'm still not enjoying myself in here, at least I don't feel like I have to watch my back all the time now. I've got far worse, far bigger problems in my life than worrying about the women in here.

Fern trumps them all.

I'm still reeling from what I heard when Greg came to visit me last week. His theory about Fern being the one who was behind everything, from plotting Drew's murder to framing me for it and then killing Rory because he knew too much, was a wild one but it actually made sense. I'd assumed Rory had framed me but, the more I think about it, the more I doubt he would have ever had the brains or the confidence to try to pull something like that off by himself. Knowing him as well as I did, there would have been far more chance of him choosing to stay with me after finding out about my affair than plotting to see me go to prison for a crime I didn't commit. He must have had help and Greg seems very sure where that help came from. It was just unfortunate for him that his partner in crime ended up turning on him, but I can't have too much sympathy there because his actions have put me in here now. But I do feel bad about the fact that without my affair in the first place, Rory would never have resorted to what he did. He was a good man and I betrayed him, leading him to team up with Fern and make a plot that, ultimately, he had to die for.

He obviously trusted Fern to go through with killing Drew and framing me, and look where it got him.

While it's good to know that I have a friend on the outside who is working hard to try and prove my innocence, it is just as worrying to think that he is going up against a truly formidable foe in Fern. The sheer audacity of pulling off a plan like she has is unbelievable, and the fact she has already gotten away with it for so long makes me think it is not going to be so easy to catch her out. Greg seems confident he can do it though, and, as far as I can tell, he's my only hope because there's not much I can do from in here. The fact he is an ex-policeman gives me hope, too – it should mean he knows what he is doing. Then again, he'd be the first because all the officers I have encountered so far have been useless; instead of arresting Drew's killer, they arrested me, so they couldn't have been more wrong there.

'Hurry up and take your shot.'

The distracting comment from the inmate behind me makes me turn around from the pool table and, when I do, I see that there are three other women waiting to use this table after Siobhan and I have finished our game. They could be waiting a while though because this is hardly my sport and potting balls is not easy at the best of times, never mind when I'm spending so much time thinking about Fern. But I heed the 'friendly suggestion' from my fellow inmate and do as she says, taking my shot and, unsurprisingly, missing it.

Thankfully, Siobhan is better than me at pool, no doubt because she has spent more time in here than me getting some practice in, so she doesn't miss as much and, as my opponent's balls are potted, I get ready to shake her hand at the end of the game and go over to one of the chairs, where I will sit until leisure time is over and we have to go back to our cells.

It's sad but playing a game of pool and sitting in that plastic chair over there are just about the highlights of my evening. To think that not so long ago, I could go wherever I wanted and see whoever I pleased. I took all that for granted, but I guess you never miss what you have until it's gone.

Drew. I think of him then as I reflect on that sentiment because that is a line that he said to me when we were lying on the bed in his surgery, after I had first found out he had moved to Arberness to be near me again. I'd tried and ultimately failed in not falling back into his arms, and after we had made love in his office after closing time, he told me he had tried to move on without me but couldn't. If only he hadn't left Manchester and followed me up north, I wouldn't be here. I'd be at home with

Rory, and while I wouldn't ever be able to honestly say that I was truly happy, it was a good life, a decent life, and a far better life than the one I deserved.

But here I am now.

I guess I got what I deserved in the end. A woman who has a loving partner should not stray, no matter how tempting things might become. Drew worked hard to make an impression on me and I fell under his spell, but I could have resisted if I had just tried that little bit harder. I owed that to my marriage. I owed it to Rory. I failed him and I failed the concept of the wedding ring on my finger, the same ring Drew eagerly ignored when he was with me.

It's easy to be full of regret in my position, but even if I was a free woman on the outside I'd still regret what I did with Drew. It wasn't right. Fate has seen to it that I've got some form of punishment for my actions.

Unfortunately, Fern has not yet got any punishment for hers and, despite what I've done wrong in life, she has me well beaten there.

'Good game,' I say to Siobhan as she pots the last ball, and I extend my hand for her to shake it. She reaches out to accept it but, as I look into her eyes, I see that she is not looking at me.

She is looking behind me and whatever she is seeing is suddenly troubling her.

'Watch out!' she cries, but it's too late because I feel a terrible pain at the back of my skull as something strikes me over the head and, as I fall backwards, I get a glimpse of my attacker standing over me.

It's Kelly and she is armed with a plastic chair. That must be what she just struck me with.

The scary thing is, she doesn't look like she is finished.

I'm right about that as she throws the chair down on top of me, causing me to howl out in pain before she gives me a strong kick in the ribs. Then she is on top of me, beating me savagely, her fists a blur as they fly in and around my face and all I can do is close my eyes, try to curl up into a ball and pray that the onslaught stops soon.

There is a brief respite when I hear Siobhan come to my aid, and I open my eyes to see my friend pushing Kelly away from me. But that only stops my main attacker, not her minions, and two of Kelly's allies quickly take her place on top of me, kicking and punching me to the point where I am certain I am going to die right here on this cold prison floor before I've had a chance at seeing justice get served.

Thank heavens for the wardens. If four of them hadn't come to my rescue then I would surely have never been able to get up off that floor again. While they might have been very slow in stopping the attack in its infancy, they eventually restore order and prevent any more damaging blows. But the injuries I have sustained are more than enough to warrant medical attention, and that is why I am taken to hospital, though I cannot see or say much on the way. I'm far too groggy for that and just opening my eyes has me closing them again quickly when the bright lights blind me. I daren't try and speak either, as I can only taste blood in my mouth; and I'm afraid to look in the mirror anytime soon. I'm almost certain to see two black eyes staring back at me when I do.

That attack came out of nowhere. I had no chance to even try and defend myself. I was so vulnerable. But that was obviously Kelly's intention. So much for her leaving me alone. I guess she just wanted to give me the illusion of being safe so I lowered my guard and, when I did, she pounced.

That woman tricked me.

She's not the only one.

By the time my injuries have been assessed by a medical professional, it's decided that I haven't suffered any broken bones and the wounds I have are superficial. I'll heal soon enough, though I'll need plenty of painkillers to be administered while I do. After tentatively making my way back to my cell, I have plenty of time to think about things as I lie on my bed and reflect on how I'm feeling. It would be easy for me to blame Kelly for my predicament. She is the one who delivered the blows to my face and body after all. But she's not the one I blame for the pain I'm in now. It is not her face that I see as I stare into the darkness and wait for the latest batch of painkillers to kick in. It is Fern's, the woman who set this whole thing in motion and ensured I was in the wrong place at the wrong time for Kelly to get her hands on me.

I'd grit my teeth as I think about her if it didn't make my jaw ache so much. Instead, all I can do is clench my fists and fantasise about getting revenge on Fern.

I'd do anything to get my own back on her but, for now, I'll just have to lie here and pray that Greg can do most of the work for me. If not, Kelly might have the chance to have another go at hurting me, and I might not survive that next assault.

SIXTEEN

FERN

So the big day has arrived. A day that is significant in any person's life. An occasion that causes one to reflect and to look forward with renewed hope. A day that can lead to crisis for some or simply celebration for others. Either way, it's usually not a day that passes without some kind of acknowledgement.

Today I turn forty.

Happy birthday to me.

While I spent all of yesterday struggling to push from my mind the fact that it was the final day I'd ever spend in my thirties, I woke up this morning feeling quite good. Perhaps I was going to be mature about reaching such a big milestone and handle it like the sensible adult my birthdate said I supposedly was. Or perhaps it had something to do with the fact that I didn't wake up alone.

I spent the entire night with Roger for the first time, and, just like reaching forty is a moment of significance, waking up in the morning beside my new man was significant in terms of our relationship. It felt good to share a bed again, to stir in the night and get the sense of comfort that came from knowing another person was lying beside me. To hear a few soft breaths on the back of my hair and to feel a strong arm wrap around my waist as the morning light filtered into the room. Most of all, to start the day with a kiss instead of the gnawing anxiety that follows a night-time of seeing Drew in my dreams and having my subconscious play tricks on my mind.

Thankfully, there were no nightmares last night, so I didn't have to explain to Roger why I woke up screaming at any point. That is a relief, not just because it keeps my secret safe, but it also ensures Roger doesn't think I'm some crazy woman and decides he never wants to spend the night with me again. Perhaps his presence was the calming influence I needed during sleep to stop me having those visions of Drew and Rory and Arberness. Maybe with him sleeping beside me, I will relax further and, before long, those bad dreams will be a thing of the past and I will sleep soundly just like I used to do before I found out Drew was cheating on me and my thoughts became filled with a need for revenge.

I'm sure looking forward to finding out because tonight we are going to be sleeping together again.

I'm currently sitting in front of the mirror in my master bedroom and applying copious amounts of makeup to my face. It's a face that doesn't necessarily have any more wrinkles on it than it did yesterday, but I am convinced it does because I've aged overnight and being forty now means I need that extra dab of concealer and one more touch of blusher. As part of the transformation that is taking place, I have had my hair styled this morning by a pricey hairdresser and I am wearing a dress I picked up on the high street on the way back, ensuring I look as good as I can do for this evening. It's only Roger who will see me, but I want to look my best for him as we check in to the hotel and get something to eat and drink in the restaurant there.

He's told me that he'll get a taxi to pick me up at seven, and a quick check on the time tells me that he'll be here any minute, so I quickly finish beautifying myself before picking up the glass of wine I poured earlier and heading downstairs.

The smell of paint is still quite strong down here, but it is fading, unlike the colours from all the bouquets of flowers I have received today from family and friends. My lounge is full of pretty petals, as it is with cards with fours and zeros on the front of them, and I take a moment to look at them all and appreciate how many people I have in my life who care about me and have wished me a happy birthday today. My parents came around for a cup of tea this afternoon, which turned into three cups of tea as it often does. Claire and a few of my other friends also made a quick visit to share a glass of prosecco with me and wish me many happy returns. All the while, I had to pretend like I was just looking forward to a quiet evening by myself tonight, not mentioning that I was actually gearing up for a romantic night in a city-centre hotel with my secret lover.

I smile when I hear the car parking up outside, and grab my coat and small overnight bag before heading out to join Roger on the backseat of the taxi. He welcomes me into the cab with a big grin and a kiss before we are on our way, passing through the city streets on our way to our home for the night.

'You look amazing,' Roger tells me, and I make sure to return the compliment before he asks me how my birthday has been so far and I tell him all about my visitors.

'So everyone thinks you're just home alone tonight?' he asks, and I confirm that is the story I have given them before hinting that it might soon be time to stop with the charade and allow him to meet a few of my loved ones. He seems happy enough to do that and we hold hands as the taxi moves on, getting us closer to our destination.

As we go, I think about how things have worked out so well and wonder just how much happier I could get over the coming months. But I'm not just thinking about all the joy that could come with introducing Roger to my parents or having him by my side at various social events with my friends.

I'm thinking about whether or not I get a positive result in the pregnancy tests that I will soon be starting to take.

After getting confirmation from Roger the other night that he was not opposed to children or indeed having them with me, I feel much better about coming off my birth control. That's why I haven't used it for the last few days and will continue to leave it alone for the foreseeable future. I haven't told the man sitting beside me in this taxi that I have stopped using contraception, but I expect that these things take time so it could be months anyway before we have any progress on the pregnancy front. Better to start trying now rather than waste time, and my birthday today reminds me that I do not have quite as much time as I'd like any more.

'Here we are. Have a lovely evening,' the taxi driver says as he parks at the front of the decadent hotel that Roger has selected for our stay this evening.

As Roger pays the fare, my door is opened by a smiling young man in a smart uniform, and he assists me in getting out of the taxi before asking if he can help with any luggage I might have. This is the kind of five-star service I would expect from an upmarket establishment like this one and, as the polite member of staff takes our bags, Roger and I follow him in to the lobby where we quickly go through the process of checking in.

I get the feeling that Roger is slightly nervous as he stands beside me and signs the forms he needs to in order to complete our room booking, but I presume that is just because he is desperately trying to ensure I have a good evening and that is very sweet of him if so. He has little to worry about on that front though, because this hotel looks incredible and I am sure the room will be too, and I'm very much looking forward to seeing it before dinner. I go to follow the bellboy to the elevators.

'Let him take the bags up. Let's go get a drink at the bar,' Roger suggests, seemingly wanting to get the evening's festivities started much sooner than I had anticipated. I'm not going to argue with his suggestion as he leads me by the hand, taking me out of the lobby and along a carpeted corridor before we reach a set of open doors at the end.

However, I can't hear any music or voices beyond it, nor can I see much inside it because it looks rather dark, and I'm just about to ask Roger if he is sure that we have gone the right way when the lights in the room suddenly come on and I see what is waiting for me in here.

'Surprise!'

I'm overwhelmed by the sight and sound of dozens of people I recognise, all of them standing around this large function room with a drink in their hands and a wide smile across their faces, happy to see that their plan has worked.

It's a surprise party, and I am most definitely surprised.

Looking to the man beside me, I see that Roger looks far less stunned than I am and that's when I realise that he is the one who has planned this whole thing, leading me here under the false pretence of a romantic night for the two of us only to have all my favourite people leap out at me at the last second.

He lied to me but, unlike the kind of lies that I was used to with Drew, I am not going to get angry about this one.

That's because this particular lie was designed to make me happy.

'I can't believe this,' I say as my parents and best friends start to head towards me to welcome me to the party that clearly started well before I got here. But then, as if the surprise of all this wasn't enough, I realise that for this to be happening, my secret must be out. Everyone must know about Roger.

But how?

It doesn't take long for me to get that answer. Roger explains just how he managed to pull this off, with the help of Claire, who I should have known had something to do with this too. It seems the pair of them have been in cahoots, and I guess I'm not the only one capable of keeping a secret. At least their secrets involve surprise parties and trays full of champagne and, as I receive my first drink of the evening, I raise my glass and thank everybody for coming tonight.

'I really wasn't expecting this,' I say honestly. 'I can't actually believe it's happening. But thank you. It's obviously been a tough year and I didn't think I would be up to something like this, which is why I said I wasn't planning anything. But I'm glad you did this for me. Oh, and by the way, everybody, this is Roger!'

Any fears I might have had about being seen to be moving on too quickly from Drew fade away amidst a tide of smiling faces, handshakes and well wishes from everybody as they come to meet my new man and tell me they are just happy that I am happy again.

I guess it is official now then, and, as I see Roger chatting with my parents, I smile to myself because this really does feel like the final link in the chain of me moving on from Drew. Finally, people will talk less about him and more about my new man and, the more that happens, the more my late husband will fade into the background. I'll still have to make the effort to go and visit his grave, as well as remember when it is his birthday or our wedding anniversary, so I can pretend to act particularly sombre on those days. But, other than that, I guess I am now free to get on with living my life, and if all these people here are as happy as they are just to meet my new boyfriend, imagine how happy they are going to be when I tell them, hopefully, that I am pregnant.

Happy birthday, indeed.

Let's get this party started.

SEVENTEEN

GREG

Considering this whole thing is an illusion, I'm actually having a good time at this party, meeting Fern's family members and friends who I have absolutely no intention of ever seeing again once this evening is complete. However, I'm definitely not having as much of a good time as the birthday girl herself. As I look at Fern across this crowded function room, I see her raising a shot glass above her head alongside five of her friends before downing her drink and letting out a triumphant cheer.

Keep drinking and keep partying, I think to myself as I watch her revelling in her popularity here amongst all these people who are yet to find out who she really is. *The more fun you have, the more likely it is that I get what I want at the end of the evening.*

'So, Roger, tell me. What do you do for work?'

I feel a hand around my shoulder and, when I see who it is, I realise I'm going to have to negotiate a conversation with Fern's father, Tony. This is always a tricky situation for any boyfriend to find himself in, getting to know the man who raised the woman he is now dating but, in my case, I'm going to have to tread even more carefully.

'I'm in sales,' I tell him, and while that might sometimes elicit a negative reaction from some people, if Tony is not impressed by that, he does a very good job of not showing it.

'Fantastic. What is it you sell?'

I spend the next five minutes boring myself as well as the man I'm talking to about the ins and outs of what it is that I do for a living these days, but while I know I could probably impress Tony a little more if I mentioned I used to be a police-man, I will keep that fact to myself. Just in case he talks about it with his daughter later and she suddenly puts up her defences, which are currently being lowered as quickly as those empty shot glasses at the bar.

'That's interesting,' Tony says, and I appreciate how polite he is being because my job is anything but that. Thankfully, he changes the subject a moment later. However, the next topic is even more tricky for me.

'I have to admit, I was a little surprised when I heard Fern had a new man in her life,' he says as the party continues around us, and I worry that this might be the part where the concerned father tells me to treat his daughter well. 'She's been through a lot, and I thought at first that it sounded like she was rushing into things when Claire told me Fern was in a relation-ship again.'

'We have been taking things slowly,' I try, but Tony cuts me off quickly.

'I'm not here to give you a warning or anything like that. I'm here to thank you.'

'Thank me?'

'Yes. My daughter deserves to be happy after what happened in the past and, even though I've only just met you, it's been clear to me for the past few months that my daughter has been coping well considering the circumstances. That tells me a lot of it is down to you, so thank you, I really appreciate you being a part of her life.'

'Oh, erm.'

I really don't know what to say to that, and just wish I didn't have to stand here and accept kind words from the father of the woman I am hoping will confess her crimes to me later this evening.

'At first, I was worried she was putting on a front with me and her mother,' Tony says, gesturing to his wife across the bar who is chatting with a couple of older relatives of the birthday girl. 'You know, pretending she wasn't suffering as much as she was just so she didn't worry her parents. But now I know there was a genuine reason why her mood wasn't as low as it could have been, and that reason is you. So thank you, Roger, and thank you for organising this party.'

Tony has his hand out to me to shake, and I know better than to leave him hanging, so I reluctantly shake it and form even more of a bond with this man who I am ultimately going to end up shocking very soon.

Tony is then very quickly pulled away to join a few family members for photos over by the bar. Once he's gone, I end up involved in yet another awkward conversation, this time with a few of Fern's friends, although quite what she sees in these people is beyond me. From what I can tell, they are very full of themselves and I'd go as far to say many of them are snobs, and that becomes even more evident after they have briefly asked me what I do for work too.

In this circle, it seems that there are only two right answers to give when it comes to questions relating to work, income and general standing in society. Either you are a doctor or you are married to a doctor. As I'm neither, I'm quickly judged, and, likewise, because Fern is no longer able to fit inside that box either, I'm judged even more, as if I am leading their dear friend away from her respectable lifestyle and down a path of boring mediocrity.

If only they knew what path I was really trying to lead her down.

'I hear sales is a terribly difficult industry to be involved in,' one friend comments as the others around nod their heads. 'Very tough to make good money there.'

'There are commissions and bonuses,' I try, attempting to make my job seem somewhat as lucrative as theirs, but then wondering why I am even bothering to try and impress these people I'll never see again after this party.

'I'm sure there are, but is it fulfilling?' someone asks me before they go on to talk about what it is like to treat sick patients and how that is truly rewarding work to be involved in.

I really want to tell them that any work can be rewarding if the person undertaking it enjoys it, but I don't want to get into a debate here, or an argument, so it's much easier to just let these people say what they want to say and keep nodding and smiling politely. I'm sure some of them are thinking that I'm not much of a match for their friend and expect our romance to fizzle out slowly over the next few months, but, if so, they would be wrong there too. Our relationship is definitely not going to fizzle out. When it ends, it is going to go out with a bang.

I excuse myself from the conversation to go and find my girl-friend and see how she is enjoying her birthday party.

I find Fern on what has become the makeshift dancefloor and, when she sees me approaching, she throws her arms around me and pulls me in to dance closely with her. It's rather a large display of affection considering this room is full of her loved ones, but it's a sign that she has no qualms about showing off how happy she is with me now. It's also a sign that she is intoxicated and, as she dances with me to the music coming from the speakers and tells me very loudly that she is having a wonderful time, I feel confident that she will soon be losing even more of her inhibitions.

The party goes on for a couple more hours, many more

drinks are consumed by the birthday girl, and I make my way through a few more tedious talks with various friends and family members before, finally, the music stops and a hotel employee politely tells us that it is time to start leaving.

As far as I know, everyone else in attendance will be going home now unless they have managed to secure themselves a room, but I definitely have a bed booked upstairs, which means Fern and I don't have far to travel before we can settle for the night, though sleep is the last thing I am planning on doing when we get there. As Fern says goodbye to those who came to help her celebrate tonight, I watch her swaying and stumbling a little and cannot wait to take advantage of that.

I cannot wait to get her talking to me in private.

'It was a pleasure to meet you,' Fern's mother, Kath, says to me before giving me a goodbye hug. I tell Kath it was great to meet her too, feeling a little melancholy as I say the words because this is clearly a lovely woman who does not deserve what is coming to her family. Her husband is just as nice and, as I shake Tony's hand and hear him invite me out for dinner with the family soon, I have to fake my smile and my answer, telling him that would be delightful and I look forward to it.

It's a relief when Fern's parents leave – I don't have to fake things with them any more. Although, their daughter is still here, so I have to keep up my act for a little while longer as I walk with her out of the now empty function room. As several cleaners pass us to go and tidy up all the empty glasses we have left behind, we head for the elevator and I push the button for the sixth floor.

As the doors slide open, Fern stumbles as she goes to get in and I grab her arm to help her keep her balance before we get inside the elevator.

'Oops,' she says before erupting in a fit of giggles, and I make sure to laugh too in order to make it seem like I am just as lightheaded and carefree as she is after all those drinks we had at the bar. But the truth is I was ordering non-alcoholic beer all night, and while I was unable to avoid the one shot of tequila that I got talked into having with Fern and a few of her friends, I am, for the most part, sober and clear-headed, and that is how I need to be as we reach our floor and head for our room. I have been clever enough to bring up a bottle of beer with me though now, swigging from it occasionally as we go back to our room, to make me appear to be just as drunk as Fern clearly is.

As I watch her walk ahead of me in the corridor, the path she takes across the carpet tells me she would easily fail the test if I was to ask her to walk in a straight line, not that she cares too much about that. She can't stop grinning, nor can she stop thanking me for organising the party. Then she gives me a long, lingering kiss just before I unlock the hotel room door and hold it open as Fern goes inside, the birthday girl singing away to herself as she enters the room.

Just before I follow her in, I say a very quiet prayer to myself, one that she won't have any chance of hearing above her singing.

'Please let this work.'

Then I do one more thing before following Fern into the room.

I take out my mobile phone and go to the video option.

Then I press record.

EIGHTEEN

FERN

Tonight has been an incredible night but, as far as I'm concerned, it's not over yet.

'Come here,' I say to Roger after he has put his phone down by the side of the bed and pulled out his shirt from where it was tucked into his smart trousers.

He seems a little caught off guard as I plant my lips on his, but I don't slow down until I have led him onto the bed and I have fallen down on top of him.

As I unbutton his shirt and fling it open, Roger rather innocently asks me what I am doing.

'The surprise party was my present,' I say as I run my hands across his bare chest. 'Now it's time for your present.'

There surely aren't many men who could resist an eager woman like me taking control of them, and Roger does not protest too much, though he does rather sweetly say we can just talk if I'd like and save anything else we are going to do for the morning. But talking is the last thing on my mind as I go for his belt buckle.

'I've spent all night talking,' I say as I throw his belt across the room and it makes a loud thud as it slaps into the wall. 'I want to do something else now.'

I put a finger to Roger's lips to tell him that he is to be quiet for the time being and, with him following my orders, I focus on him. It feels good to be doing this after the wonderful evening he has arranged for me.

To say the surprise party was an actual surprise would be an understatement. I had no idea what was waiting for me when we walked into that room, and genuinely believed Roger and the original plan he had told me about before we got here. But to see all my family and friends there and realise the effort my new man had gone to in organising the celebration was incredible. Any doubts I had about slowly and quietly introducing him to my loved ones were quickly dispelled when I realised how much fun the party was going to be.

While I'd asked for a quiet night, deep down, I know I would have regretted not marking my fortieth birthday in style in years to come. I've never been someone who likes to lurk in the shadows and let big occasions pass without much of a mention, and was only behaving in this way because of Drew's death. But, even in my attempts to keep things lowkey, it seems the universe had other ideas for me, or rather my new boyfriend did.

What a guy he is.

With my secret out, I suppose I will have to start organising all sorts of things with Roger by my side now. Meals with my parents. Double dates with my friends. I guess I'll have to go and meet his loved ones too. There's no doubt it is going to be a busy time in our relationship now so many people are aware of it. But that's okay. Everyone tonight was happy because I was happy, and not a single one of them mentioned Drew or raised any concerns about me moving on too quickly. I guess that's love and loyalty for you. Everyone in that room this evening only wanted what is best for me.

Right now, I only want what is best for Roger.

As I work on making him as happy as I am, I haven't yet let it slip that I have stopped using birth control. I don't want to ruin the moment by suddenly mentioning something that could be quite serious but, on the other hand, we have already discussed kids and there was no issue there, so what's the big deal? I'm hardly likely to conceive this early, if at all, and even if I do I doubt Roger will be able to pinpoint the exact time of conception. We certainly do this kind of thing enough to make it hard to remember the exact date. I'll tell him about my decision to come off birth control soon, sometime this week, but tonight it's time for having fun.

As Roger and I make love, I seem to be doing most of the work but I put that down to two things. One, my desire to reward him for his efforts earlier and, two, my boundless energy in comparison to him after all the drinks I had downstairs with my loved ones. I've definitely overdone it at the bar this evening and I know that because every time I raise my head up and look around this hotel room, a few of the walls seem to start moving and I could swear the carpet gets closer to me every now and again too. But so what if I'm drunk? I'm only forty once and, besides, there aren't many people who can resist partaking when everyone wants to buy them a free drink.

After an energetic twenty minutes or so, Roger and I find ourselves lying on our pillows staring into each other's eyes and, as our breathing returns to normal, my eyelids are already starting to grow heavy. It's late, I've had a lot to drink, and the dopamine hit I just received from what I did with Roger is slowly starting to wear off.

Time to say goodnight.

Before I can, Roger starts talking.

'Now that we're official, I think we should start sharing more things with each other,' he says.

'Like what?' I ask, my mind on sleep but being polite

enough to humour him for a moment.

'Anything. Good things, bad things. Like tonight for example.'

'What about tonight?'

'I had fun, don't get me wrong. But I also felt a bit like some of your friends were judging me.'

'Judging you?'

'Yeah, because I'm not a doctor like some of them are. Or like Drew was.'

'They weren't judging you,' I say, hoping that is correct but, even if they were, I presume they weren't too rude about it.

'They were. I don't think they were that impressed when I told them I was a salesman.'

'They were just being nosey. Nobody really cares what anybody does for a living. It's just a topic of conversation at a party.'

'I suppose.'

I am ready to close my eyes and allow my fuzzy brain to take me into sleep, but I resist for a little longer because I detect that Roger is feeling a bit melancholy.

'Hey, seriously, don't worry about it. Even if they were judging you, so what? All that matters is that I love you and I couldn't care less what other people think.'

'So you don't mind that I'm not some bigshot doctor?'

'No, of course not! In fact, I prefer it.'

'You do?'

'Yeah. That profession is overrated. Sometimes all that power and respectability goes to people's heads. It certainly went to Drew's.'

Annoyingly, even after a perfect evening, there's always room for thoughts of that man to creep in.

'You think his job had something to do with his affair?'

'Probably. He was overconfident. Cocky. Thought he could do whatever he wanted because he'd had a lifetime of people admiring him, deferring to him, trusting him. Everyone trusts a doctor, don't they? He certainly took advantage of that.'

I still want to go to sleep, but discussing Drew has suddenly stirred up a little anger and resentment inside me and I think that makes fully relaxing a little harder as a result.

'I guess,' Roger says, looking sleepy himself but still talking anyway. 'It's funny because I'm sure even after what he did, most of those people at the party tonight still think he was a good guy.'

'Probably,' I mutter, annoyed if that is the case. 'But I knew what he was like and that's all that matters.'

There's a moment of quiet then, and I suspect this might be the time we both slip into sleep. But then Roger goes and says something that wakes me.

'I love you,' he mutters quietly, totally catching me off guard, but in a good way.

'I love you too,' I say, almost saying it back to him before I've really had chance to think about it. But it's true. I do love him. Tonight just confirmed it.

With those sentiments shared, I smile as I snuggle closer into Roger, basking in the affirmation that our relationship has just ascended to a whole new level. That ascension becomes even more apparent when Roger tells me he has a regret about a previous partner of his.

'I hate what Drew did to you because I know what it's like. I've been cheated on too,' he says, which is a surprise to me because he has never mentioned this before, though I can tell it's because he feels self-conscious about it. 'And I'm not angry at her any more. I gave that up a long time ago. But I am angry at myself.'

'Yourself? Why?'

'I don't know. Because I trusted her. Because I allowed myself to get walked over.'

'Her cheating is not your fault. Never blame yourself.'

'Yeah, I suppose. I guess the thing I'm most angry at myself for is different.'

'What do you mean?'

'I'm angry because I didn't deal with it well. I guess I wish that I'd got my own back... Does that make sense?'

'It does,' I say, totally understanding why he might feel that way because I'm sure that if I hadn't got revenge on Drew then I'd be angry as well.

'Do you feel the same way?' Roger asks me then. 'I mean, because Drew died before you ever got to even talk to him about it?'

I think about just agreeing with him there, but I can see he's hurting and wants to hear something that might cheer him up, plus I'm feeling super confident after he has just told me he loves me, so I decide it can't do any harm to let on that I did actually get my own back on Drew.

'Don't worry, I did what I had to,' I say, unable to resist a smug smile spreading across my face.

'What do you mean?'

'I got revenge on him, don't worry about that.'

'But how? He died before you knew he was having an affair.'

'Did he?'

I should shut up but it's delicious to revel in my victory and, finally, I'm letting somebody in on how clever I have been. It's okay because it's somebody I can trust. Somebody who loves me. Somebody who has been hurt by another person before. He needs to know that victims of cheating are not always powerless.

'You found out about his affair before he died?' Roger asks me, not seemingly surprised, just genuinely curious. But this conversation won't go further than this pillow, so I am happy to keep going.

'Yes,' I say.

'How?'

'Oh, Drew was not as good at covering his tracks as he thought he was. Neither was she. *Alice.*'

I detest saying her name. I shouldn't, though, because I'm in a spacious hotel room bed while she is on an uncomfortable mattress in prison.

'What do you mean?' Roger asks as he tucks a strand of my hair behind my ear.

'Her partner found out about her affair too. Rory. He was the one who told me about it. He'd followed them and seen them together. Then he came and told me.'

'Wow, in Arberness?'

'No, in Manchester.'

Roger does look surprised now, but I just shrug because, feeling as good as I do, it's not as if it's very important.

'Wait, if you knew about the affair, why did you move to Arberness?' he asks me next.

'To test him,' I say. 'I wanted to see if he would do the right thing and stay away from *her* when we got there. But he didn't. I heard them having sex in his office. Right there on the bed where he treats his patients. Can you believe the gall of him to do that?'

'That's disgusting,' Roger agrees, clearly on my side. 'What a horrible man.'

'He was the worst,' I confirm.

'I still don't understand,' Roger says then. 'I thought you said you got your own back on him. But how? Alice killed him, didn't she?'

'Did she?' I ask, smiling again.

'She didn't?'

'Let's just say that I didn't just get revenge on Drew. I got revenge on her too.'

I wait a moment for Roger to piece it together and when he does, he laughs.

'Wow, you killed him and framed her? That's genius!'

Maybe if I was sober then I'd regret letting such a thing slip, but as it is I'm feeling very merry and, even if I wasn't, Roger seems to have no problem with what I have done, so I confirm it.

'Yes,' I say. 'Well kind of. I had help. But it was my idea to get back at them. Does that make me a bad person?'

'No, of course not. They deserved it!'

'I think so too,' I say.

'What about that other guy? Alice's husband? Is that who helped you?'

'Yes. He was being cheated on too, so it was quite easy to get him on side.'

'But what happened with him?'

'What do you mean?'

'I heard he killed himself.'

'He didn't kill himself.'

'He didn't?'

'Let's just say he could have been a problem for me, but isn't any more.'

I feel the need to stop talking now because I've said far more than I should have done, but I'm feeling exhilarated to have Roger in on my secret and, knowing that he is fully on my side, I roll back on top of him and start kissing him again. He kisses me back too, more passionately than he has ever done before, and the sex that follows is our best yet.

I guess letting him in on my little secret wasn't such a bad thing to do.

He clearly loves me, even with what I have done in my past.

I guess it also helps that he knows better than to ever think about cheating on me himself.

He knows what would happen if he was to do that, so I doubt he'll even try.

Perfect. I got rid of a disloyal man and found myself a loyal one.

Who said turning forty has to be bad?

NINETEEN
GREG

I wonder if Fern noticed a big difference in me when we slept together before turning out the lights and settling down for the night. If she did, she probably put it down to me just being more attentive and engaged now that we have both said the 'L' word to each other. She'll have no idea that the real reason I was far more enthusiastic with her was because I was so exhilarated after she had just given me the evidence I needed.

I feel so happy to have finally got her confession and, now I have it, I can get justice for two people I care about: Drew and Alice. The truth can come out about what happened to my late friend in his final moments and that is all anybody deserves when they lose their life in such an awful way. On top of that, I hope Alice's conviction can be overturned now, and the police can finally start looking in the direction of the person who is really responsible.

That person is currently fast asleep beside me in this bed and, as I lie here wide awake in the dark and listen to Fern's breathing, I am still struggling to control the adrenaline pumping through my body. Knowing that sleep is impossible for me, not just because I'm excited but also wary now I have confirmation that I am in the presence of a deceptive killer, I ever so carefully get out of bed, making sure not to disturb Fern. Then I pick up my phone from the bedside table, the one I have been too nervous to look at since I set it down and left it recording, before I quietly make my way into the bathroom and lock the door behind me.

Taking a very deep breath, I allow myself a moment to try and decompress before I look down at the phone in my hands. This is it. The moment of truth. The time when I find out if I successfully managed to get the recording of Fern admitting she knew about Drew's affair before his death and saw to it that all involved got what she felt they deserved.

I'm full of anticipation when I tap the screen and see that the seconds are still counting, indicating that the recording is still underway, not that I need to record anything more. Fingers crossed I have all I need, so I hit the pause button before going back to the beginning and, after making sure the volume is just loud enough for me to hear it, I press play.

I hear nothing for a few seconds and almost start panicking that something hasn't worked as it should have.

But then I hear Fern's voice.

She's talking about what a good time she had this evening and then I hear myself say how nice it was to meet her parents, and I relax because now it's clear the phone was in range to easily pick up both of our voices. Knowing that we chatted for a little while about things that aren't pertinent to my 'investigation', I move my finger across the bar at the bottom of the recording to make it skip forward until I get to around when I think our conversation really got interesting. That's when I hear myself leading Fern into the trap I was setting for her, talking about being judged by some of Fern's friends and how I felt that they didn't respect my job as much as they did Drew's.

I keep the phone close to my ear as I listen to the recording on low volume, wary of Fern overhearing anything, even though she is on the other side of this locked door and was asleep when I left her a moment ago. I haven't come this far to make a stupid mistake now and ruin everything.

After hearing Fern and myself make declarations of love to each other, a thing that would make me nauseous if it wasn't so laughable, I hear myself tell another lie. This time, it's the one about an ex-partner cheating on me before, a fib I told to further engender Fern's love and sympathy but also to lead her down the track of talking about the best way to get revenge on cheaters. Sure enough, I hear her telling me that none of it was my fault and, after I tell another lie about how I regret not getting my own back on those who wronged me in the past, Fern begins to confess what she did to Drew and Alice.

I hold my breath and grit my teeth as I pray that the audio recording of the next part is crystal clear. I'd hate for some well-paid defence lawyer to find a way of discrediting what ended up being Fern's confession. But there is no need for such worries because the audio is perfect – I hear Fern's voice clearly as she says several very incriminating things.

'I got revenge on him, don't worry about that.'

'Let's just say that I didn't just get revenge on Drew. I got revenge on her too.'

I then hear myself ask the very crucial question.

'Wow, you killed him and framed her?'

That is followed by one very short but very important word from Fern.

'Yes.'

There's so much here that any police officer, detective or prosecutor could have a field day with and, as I listen to it all in its entirety, I am convinced there is no way Fern will be able to wriggle out of this one. If I was to guess, I'd say her best defence would be to say that she was drunk and was just making things up, but surely that won't fool anybody or excuse the things she is saying. What it will do is make everybody investigate her and, with the full gaze of the justice system upon her, my plan is that she will crumble under the spotlight and the rest of the process will be a formality.

She'll be charged. Stand trial if she still denies it. Be found guilty by a jury who have listened to the recording and can't believe what they heard. She will be given a very long prison sentence for everything she has done wrong. And then this will all be over.

Barely able to contain my excitement, I find myself pacing around the small bathroom, unable to take more than three or four steps in one direction before I have to turn back and walk the other way again. But I'm also unable to stand still and that is why I keep moving around with the phone in my hand and my thoughts racing through my brain at a million miles per hour. In the end, I have to close the toilet seat lid and sit down on it just to stop myself bursting with pent-up emotion, but even sitting, I still find it difficult to stay calm.

What has just happened is the result of months of me dedicating my life to trying to get the truth, and there were many times that I didn't think it was ever going to amount to anything. The fears I had as I went to bed at night in my flat were that I was wasting my time, that maybe I was wrong, or worst of all that Fern was simply too clever to ever make a mistake around me. They were such palpable worries that I'd often wake in the middle of the night with my heart racing, a troubling symptom that occurred when I was a police officer and was one of the many reasons I ultimately decided to leave that line of work. There were even a couple of times when I felt like giving up with Fern because I worried I was chasing a lost cause. But I kept going, motivated by the sense of justice I had instilled in me during my police career, because it wasn't all bad, as well as a deep desire to get the truth for Drew's family and also see Alice back on the outside, where she might find herself falling into the arms of the man who helped save her from a lifetime of custody.

It's all been worth it.

I've done it.

Now it's time to get out of here.

Eager to get away from Fern and to never see her again, my plan is to quietly leave this bathroom, grab a few items of clothing before sneaking out of the room and going downstairs. When I'm in the lobby, I will ask whoever is on the reception desk to call the police and, when they get here, I will lead them back up to this room where they can surprise the sleeping criminal and put handcuffs on her before she has time to do anything about it.

I imagine that's when things will slow down a little bit because, as eager as I am for things to happen quickly, the wheels of the British legal system turn slowly, and it could be a while before Fern is actually convicted and Alice is officially released. But so be it. The important thing is that I get those wheels turning and they will certainly be doing that when all of Fern's crimes are laid bare for everybody to hear.

Getting up from the toilet seat, I put my phone in my pocket and take one more deep breath before reaching out for the lock on the door and preparing to slide it open as quietly as I can. But just before I do that, I hear a sound that makes me freeze.

It's a knock on the bathroom door.

TWENTY

FERN

Despite having one of the most memorable nights of my life, I can't say that I am feeling my best as I stand outside the bathroom door and wait to hear how Roger is doing on the other side of it.

I haven't been asleep for long and still feel drunk if I'm honest, although the warm, fuzzy effects of all the alcohol have started to wear off a little bit by now and in their place are the first beginnings of what is going to be an almighty hangover. I have a headache, my throat is impossibly dry and I already know that whatever sleep I end up getting for the rest of the night will not be quality, and I'm likely to be feeling fatigued all day tomorrow. That's just the price I pay for celebrating my fortieth in such style though, and I'm a big girl so I can handle it. However, I am worried about my boyfriend because I've woken up and he's not in the bed beside me, and as I try the bathroom door to find it is locked, I worry he is suffering more than I am after tonight's celebrations.

'Are you okay? Are you being sick?' I ask Roger before listening out for his response.

'No, I'm okay. I just needed the toilet,' comes the reply, but

I'm not sure he's being entirely honest, because if I was sick, I wouldn't really want to admit it either.

'Are you sure?'

'Yeah, fine. Thanks. Go back to bed. I'll be out in a minute,' he replies.

I decide that I'd rather spend that minute lying on the bed than standing by the doorway, so I stagger back towards the mattress and prepare to fall back into the welcoming warmness of the duvet. But, just before I do, I scoop up my handbag from where I must have thrown it on the floor and search for the headache tablets I keep in there. I find them quickly enough, but I know it will take a little more time before their effects are felt in my body.

Gulping down two pills and taking a swig of water from my bottle, I tell myself that I have made a good start on staving off some of my impending hangover before I take my phone from my bag and then crawl back into bed.

Gaining some temporary relief now that I'm horizontal again, I peruse social media for a moment. I have the morbid urge to make another check on an 'old friend'. Typing *Alice Richardson* into the search engine, I am expecting to get the same thing I got last time I searched for this name, which is no new results of any relevancy to me. But I am wrong because the first thing I see is a link to an article that I instantly know refers to the woman I framed for murder.

Doctor Killer Attacked in Prison – Alice Richardson Beaten by Fellow Inmate

Shocked and eager to know more, I click on the link and am taken to a news website that is recognisable to me but hardly respectable. This is not a national news carrier, the type that triple checks their facts before putting something into print. Instead, this is the website run by an intrepid and somewhat trashy journalist called Miles Mayhew, which I suspect is not his real name. That's not all I suspect of being fake, because Miles's website is full of all sorts of news stories that say all sorts of speculative things, things he would never get away with saying at a reputable media company with a legally minded editor overseeing his work. I've read his work before, because he is based in the far north of England and seems to cover any big stories that occur on this side of the border or just over it in Scotland. That puts him in prime territory for Arberness and Carlisle, which are the places of interest for the murder of Drew Devlin and all that came after it.

I consumed a couple of articles by Miles in the early months after Drew's death, reading his reports about the investigation, Alice's arrest and subsequent conviction, and, of course, Rory's death and the fact that the police were satisfied there were no suspicious circumstances there. What Miles might be lacking in actual journalistic qualifications, he seems to make up for in sheer enthusiasm and a hunger to report on things the fastest, which might make him liable to be sued one day but, in the meantime, ensures he is often first to a story. It seems he is first to this one because he is the only one reporting on Alice being attacked in prison so far.

While the bigger media sites might not deem this particular story newsworthy, I am desperate to find out more so I read the article as quickly as I can to ascertain all the facts, or at least what can be considered close to them. From Miles's report, it seems Alice was beaten up in an ambush while in custody and, while she did not suffer any broken bones, her injuries were severe enough to require her to receive some medical care.

I could feel one of two ways after learning of such a thing. I could feel incredibly guilty that an innocent woman has been badly beaten up in prison after I helped put her there. Or I could feel satisfied that it is just more bad luck being dealt out to a woman who had no problem sleeping with my husband before her sins were exposed.

I guess the big wide grin on my face tells me which one I have gone with.

Warmed by the thought of Alice's pretty face covered in bruises, I forget that I am still waiting for Roger to come back out of the bathroom and, instead, find myself seeing what else Miles has written about recently on here.

That's how I see the link to another recent article about Alice Richardson that I have not seen before, and the headline is certainly click-worthy.

Killer Gets Visit from Mystery Man – Who is the Handsome Guy Keeping Alice Richardson Company in Prison?

I assume Miles has been hanging around outside the prison to get a 'scoop' like this one, but credible journalism's loss is my gain, because his intrepid work has given me the opportunity to find out about this.

Intrigued to know who might have been visiting Alice, I click the link, assuming I'm going to read an article about some weirdo who has become obsessed with Alice in the news, who has been visiting the condemned woman to offer some form of support. If so, that would make Alice's plight even more pathetic than it already is: she will have gone from a woman who could snare herself a handsome doctor to one who has to depend on the needy men in society, who prey on incarcerated woman for their own selfish needs. But that is not what I get at all. When I see the photo of the man who has been visiting Alice, I sit bolt upright in bed and almost drop my phone in shock.

It takes me several seconds before I can pluck up the courage to look back at my phone after almost losing my grip on it, but I must do because I have to doublecheck what I thought I just saw.

I have to be mistaken.

I can't have just seen who I thought I did, can I?

It has to just be somebody who looks like him.

Then I look back at my phone and realise I am not wrong.

I saw correctly the first time.

I know who Alice's visitor is.

The man in the image on my screen is the man who was just lying beside me in this dark hotel room.

TWENTY-ONE

FERN

It seems I've just discovered the secret of how to sober up instantly. I'm no longer feeling drunk or dishevelled after my exploits at the party earlier. Instead, I'm as wide awake as I have ever been, as I leap out of bed and try to figure out what the hell is going on.

The man in the photo featured in the online article is Roger, which means he has been to visit Alice in prison.

Why? How does he know her? What business could he possibly have with Alice?

They are all questions I am desperate to know the answer to, but there is one overriding question that trumps all else.

Is Roger really on my side?

Or is he on hers?

I'm pacing around the messy hotel room and trying not to be sick. My nausea has nothing to do with anything I've consumed and everything to do with what I have just seen and read. Going back to the article, I read the report, which tells me that this man visited Alice during regular visiting hours at Carlisle prison, and while the man's identity was not known to

Miles, the photo the journalist took is more than enough for me to identify him.

While Miles's report is eager to explore the possibility that Alice had another lover on the outside before her arrest, one in addition to both her husband and mine, I am just as eager to know the truth too. Is that what this is? Was Alice also sleeping with Roger before she was arrested? If so, that would mean he has feelings for her, and visiting her in prison proves it.

But if he loves her, why the hell is he with me?

It feels like the walls of this hotel room are closing in on me as I try to figure this all out before Roger comes out of the bathroom. And I need to, otherwise I am going to be caught very off guard, and that can't be a good thing.

I usually pride myself on staying composed in moments of stress. I did it when I found out about Drew's affair; I did it when the police came to question me after his body was found; and I did it when I realised Rory was struggling to keep our secret hidden, and had to be taken care of before I left Arberness for good. If I could do all that then I can manage this, so I force myself to stop pacing and take several deep breaths, sucking in the stale air in this stuffy room, before I compose myself and tell myself to think.

What is Roger doing here?

If he knows Alice then he has to know my history with her. It also means that if he is visiting her he must be sympathetic to her plight. He must be either an old friend or a lover, unless she has a brother I didn't know about it. Whatever the reason for his visit, it tells me he has to be supportive of her, which in turn must mean he is *against* me. Why else would he be dating the widow of the doctor who Alice went to prison for killing? It just doesn't make sense.

So he's been deceiving me. Keeping secrets from me.

But has he been working against me?

My head is aching, but it's more to do with how much brain

power I am putting in trying to solve this puzzle. However, the more I think about it, the worse I feel, because I fear I have been betrayed. I just told Roger I loved him, and he said the same thing back. But how can he love me if he has a connection with Alice? Do the two of them know what I have done? Did he get closer to me to try and catch me out? No, surely not.

That's when my alcohol-amnesia fog lifts and I remember exactly what I told Roger before I went to sleep.

It's as if time stands still as I recall my conversation with him. How I told him I knew about Drew's affair sooner than everyone thought I did and, more importantly, how I then did something to get my own back. I confessed to being involved in Drew's murder and framing Alice, and not only that but I admitted that Rory had been a problem for me so I got rid of him too.

Oh my God, I told Roger everything.

That was when I thought he was on my side.

That was before I knew he was close with *her*.

The more I think back over what we talked about, the more I remember what I said and that's when I realise Roger induced so much of what I told him. He led me along and steered the conversation to where he wanted it to go. He got me talking about Drew and secrets and regrets and must have known that I was drunk and more liable to say something I might later wish I hadn't.

He played me and that's when I see that this whole night – this whole relationship – must have been a sham. The surprise party and telling me he loved me. Did he do all this tonight just to get me drunk and to make me fall in love with him? Did he think that by making such a romantic gesture to me that it would increase the chances of me slipping up and saying something stupid? If so, it worked.

But I don't get it. How could Roger know what I did with Drew, Alice and Rory before I told him? What made him suspicious? Did Alice tell him she suspected me? If so, why didn't she just say that to the police? As far as I know, she hasn't done that because they have never been back to question me since she was charged with Drew's murder. The last time I spoke to the police in a formal type of interview, it was before there was any prime suspect in his death. They've left me alone since they zeroed in on Alice, which told me that neither the police nor Alice had any idea I was the one who put her in prison. If that's the case, how could Roger have possibly figured out I was guilty? I have no idea, but I have to assume he is working against me, and now it seems I have yet another enemy.

This cannot be happening. Am I still asleep? Is this a bad dream? Another nightmare? If so, I really hope Drew makes an appearance soon to confirm it. I'd be happy to see his bloody face right in front of me, if it meant none of this was real. Unfortunately, no matter how much I look around the hotel room and search for a sight of my dead husband, I do not see him. The only thing that happens is I hear the toilet flush in the bathroom, and it reminds me that the man who has been keeping secrets from me is still in there. But he can't stay in there forever. He has to come out sometime and, when he does, what do I do?

It seems as if it would be a bad idea for me to start panicking and asking him questions as soon as he leaves the bathroom, because that will only heighten this situation. At the moment, he won't know that I know he went to see Alice. He's kept that quiet from me for a reason, but I can do the same to him. He has his secrets and I have mine. What I need to do is stay calm and try and stay one step ahead of him. I need to figure out my next move while studying him, and see if he gives me any clues as to what he plans to do with what I told him.

I hear the tap running in the bathroom. He must be washing his hands. He's certainly been in there a while. Did he really get out of bed just to go to the toilet? Or did he go in there because he was trying to process what I told him earlier? Is he figuring out what to do with my secrets? Is he excitedly preparing to leave this room and go and tell Alice and the police what he heard, so that she can be released and I can be arrested?

Fearing that is the case, I know what I must do. I must not allow Roger to leave this room until I have figured out the extent of his plan. That's why, as I hear the bathroom door unlock, I step towards it and, when Roger appears, I offer my hand to him.

'Hey babe. Are you okay?' I ask him, taking his hand and holding on to it to make it harder for him to get out of the bedroom.

'Err, yeah. I'm fine,' he says.

'Good. Let's get back into bed then and snuggle.'

I lead him towards the bed then, but he seems reluctant to follow and he asks me if I need to go to the bathroom myself.

'No, I'm okay. Let's just go back to sleep,' I say, and I pull him back down onto the bed with me.

His body is stiff and tense, which suggests he really doesn't want to be here any more, and only makes me determined to keep him here. As we lie back on the mattress, I put my arm over him. It looks like I'm snuggling him and being affectionate but that's only because I want it to look that way. In reality, Roger is now pinned down and I'm hoping that, by being in this position, and with it being so late, he will find it hard to resist dropping off to sleep soon.

'Let's get some rest,' I say, whispering in his ear, and Roger reluctantly goes along with my plan, putting his phone down on the bedside table before saying goodnight to me and rolling over.

I keep my eyes open and stare at his back to make sure that he doesn't move, and I'm willing to stay like this all night if I have to just to ensure he doesn't sneak out of this bed again. He doesn't make a move and, after watching him for several very long minutes, I hear what sounds like light snoring.

With Roger asleep, I allow myself to relax just a little; it seems I have managed to buy myself some more time to figure this out. However, I am still unsure what to do and spend several more minutes trying to ascertain what Roger's goal was here. Okay, so he successfully induced a confession from me, one that would be very damaging if the police were to have heard it too. But they didn't. It was just between me and him. Pillow talk amongst two lovers at the end of a long night. If that's all Roger has, good luck getting that to stick, because it'll just be his word against mine and I can deny such a conversation ever took place.

Unless he secretly recorded it.

My heart skips a beat when I think about Roger or, more specifically, Roger's mobile phone. Is that what he has done? Has he used his phone to record my confession? If so, he has everything he needs to ruin me.

Looking past him, I see his phone on the bedside table and stare at it for several stressful seconds, desperate to know if there is a recording on that device that could see me spend the rest of my life in prison. But, of course, there is no way for me to know if there is or not unless I actually take a look for myself.

Can I do that? It's incredibly risky. What if Roger wakes up and sees me? He'll know I suspect him of something then and the game will be up. What happens then? Would he try and hurt me to keep that recording safe?

I know I cannot trust this man or try to predict any of his future moves after what I have learnt tonight, but I'm also aware that I'll never really know for sure what he has on me unless I look for myself. That's why I have to check his phone while he sleeps.

Gritting my teeth and tensing every muscle in my body, I attempt to get up off the bed as quietly as I can, terrified of moving the mattress enough to stir Roger from his slumber. I somehow manage it, but, even once I'm on my feet, I still have to creep around the bed to get to his phone.

I can hear my own heartbeat thudding away in my body as I take several tentative steps in the direction of Roger's bedside table and, when I get there, I slowly reach out for his phone. I'm imagining him shooting out a hand to stop me and that would surely make me scream if he was to do that, but thankfully, he does not move. With his phone now in my possession, I just need to get it unlocked so I can see what he has on it and, thanks to Face ID, all I have to do is hold it in front of him as he sleeps and it unlocks the device.

With full access now, I turn away from Roger and quickly go in search of any evidence he might have on here. My first port of call is his camera app where any recordings would be kept, and I'm hoping the only thing I will see here that is recent are several photos Roger might have taken at the party. Sure enough, there are a few images of the party, mostly of me posing with groups of my friends. But then my world comes crashing down when I see the last thing he has saved on here.

It is a video that appears to be several minutes' long.

There is no image with it, just a black screen, so that suggests it was taken when the lights were out and that only makes me more afraid that this recording occurred when we were talking in bed. There's only one way to find out for sure, so, with bated breath, I hover my finger over the play button and prepare to learn the extent of the trouble I am in.

But just before I can press play and listen to the recording, I hear something behind me.

There's movement on the bed.

Roger is not asleep at all.

TWENTY-TWO

FERN

'Put the phone down, Fern,' Roger says to me as I spin around and find him watching me.

He's already fooled me once before and now it seems he has fooled me again. He wasn't asleep, he just wanted me to think he was, probably to test me and see if I was on to him.

Now he knows I am, what is he going to do about it?

'Fern, give it here,' he says again and, this time, he lunges for the phone, but I swipe it away from him and rush across the room to create more space between us. Unfortunately, he is quickly out of bed and closing that gap again.

Thinking fast, I grab his empty beer bottle from the side and hold it out in front of myself.

'Stay back!' I urge him, and Roger does as I say, surely well aware that I'm not the kind of woman he should test the patience of.

'Fern, calm down. What are you doing? I thought we were going to sleep,' he says, his eyes still on the bottle.

'Tell me what is going on! Tell me what you are doing!' I demand to know.

'What are you talking about?'

'I'm talking about everything! Why are you with me? What are you trying to do?'

'I'm not trying to do anything. Relax. Come back to bed.'

'No! You recorded our conversation, didn't you?!'

'What conversation?'

'The one we just had. The one in which I told you about Drew!'

There is a flicker of emotion on Roger's face before he goes back to acting again.

'Fern, I think you've misunderstood. Just give me my phone back and let's talk about this in the morning.'

'No, I want to talk about it now!' I cry, thrusting the bottle towards him again and making sure he stays out of its reach if he knows what's good for him.

With Roger staying back, I have time then to do what I wanted to do thirty seconds ago. I press play on the video and listen to what it has recorded.

Hearing my voice clearly, I stare at Roger before I hear his too.

'Fern, listen to me,' he says, his hands out in front of himself as if trying to pacify me. But that is not going to work, and certainly not when I realise that he has clearly recorded every single thing I said to him in what I thought was strict confidentiality.

He has it all here.

He has me admitting to everything.

'Why have you done this?' I ask him. 'Why did you record our private conversation?'

'It doesn't matter.'

'What do you mean *it doesn't matter*? Of course it does!'

I've had enough of him stalling and, to prove it, I hit the bottom of the bottle against the table beside me, cutting it in half, meaning what is left of it in my hands is now a very sharp and dangerous weapon.

As Roger stares at the jagged edges of the broken bottle, I tell him what I just found out.

'I know you went to see Alice in prison,' I say. 'How do you know her? What is your relationship with her?'

Roger looks surprised by my admission and seems to be racking his brains to discover how I could have possibly found out about such a thing.

'That's right. I know all about it. What business could you have going to visit that woman?'

'Fern...'

'You have two seconds to tell me the truth or I swear I will use this bottle,' I warn, and I raise the sharp object above my head to prove that I mean it.

'Fine, okay! Just calm down. Yes, I went to see Alice.'

'Why?'

'I just did.'

'Was it about me?'

'What? No.'

'Then why?'

'I don't know.'

'You think she's innocent, don't you? You're trying to get her out of prison. That's what all of this is about, isn't it? That's why you're with me. You've been tricking me.'

'No.'

'Tell the truth!'

I make a large slashing motion in Roger's direction, and the bottle narrowly avoids cutting his hands as he holds them up to defend himself.

'Wait!' he cries, and now it looks like he has realised the truth is the only thing that is going to help him here. 'Okay, fine. I admit it. Yes, I have been trying to help Alice.'

There it is. Confirmation that even though she is in a prison cell miles away from here, that woman still haunts me.

'This was all a lie? Us? Everything you said to me? You were just pretending?'

Roger slowly nods his head.

'I don't understand,' I say before I think back to the first time I met him. How he approached me in that bar. How he initiated the conversation. How it seemed to be just a chance meeting between two people who would go on to fall in love, a meeting no different to how so many other relationships start. But it wasn't. It was all a fraud. *And I fell for it.*

'Why you?' I ask him then. 'What has this got to do with you? Why get involved with me? Did you know Alice before all of this?'

Roger surprises me then by shaking his head.

'So what's your connection then?' I ask him.

'Drew,' he replies quietly.

I did not see that coming, and Roger tries to take advantage of my momentary shock. He steps towards me, but I quickly raise the bottle again and he abruptly stops.

'How did you know Drew?' I ask him.

'We played tennis together,' he replies, and that's when I realise this is the mystery friend my husband went out to meet many times before we moved to Arberness. It's funny but, after I found out about Drew's affair, I often wondered if the tennis friend even existed at all, or if it might have just been an excuse Drew gave me so he could go and see Alice or maybe even another woman. But now I see that the tennis games were real, and Drew was playing with Roger all that time.

But wait a minute...

'He told me his friend was called Greg,' I say before it takes me a couple of seconds to catch up and realise Roger is a fake name. 'No? You're Greg?'

Greg nods and the last bit of the illusion that was my boyfriend, Roger, evaporates before my very eyes.

I can't believe I've been so gullible. So easily led. I've gone from thinking I had met my future husband to finding out he was an even bigger liar than my last one.

'You met all my family and friends!' I cry. 'I introduced you! All that time, you were just pretending?'

Greg nods nervously, but I suspect he is only nervous because I am still holding the bottle and not because he feels bad for breaking my heart or for getting me to be physical with him under false pretences, which is a crime. If he doesn't feel bad for that, I am not going to feel bad about what I do to him next.

I would love nothing more than to plunge this broken bottle into the stomach of the lying man standing in front of me, but I stop myself. I have to think how this would look. I can't just kill him and expect to get away with, can I? What good would it be if I had got away with my crimes in the past only to slip up and get arrested for another very serious one right here? I can't just stab Greg and, unfortunately for me, Greg seems to have just realised that too.

'Don't do anything stupid,' he says to me. 'You'll never get away with it. Just put the bottle down and let's talk.'

I'm not quite ready to do that yet, though I am ready to do something else.

I'm going to delete this video.

As I move my finger over the delete button on the phone, Greg rushes towards me and, in my shock, I drop the bottle and the phone.

'It's over!' he tells me as he goes for the phone, and while I try to drag him away from it, it's no good because he is stronger than me. All I can do is try and cling on to his arm. He just uses his free hand to turn and strike me, sending me falling backwards on to the carpet.

The blow he struck has me seeing stars and it takes me several seconds that I don't have to recover from it. When I do, I see that Greg has his phone back in his possession and is now running for the door. I realise that if he gets through it before I can stop him then this is all over, and I will be in handcuffs within the hour. That's why I grab the bottle and give chase and, just as Greg has his hand on the door, I pounce, plunging the bottle into the side of his neck and causing a huge spurt of blood to erupt.

As I stare in horror at all the red liquid now on the wall by the door, Greg stumbles backwards with one hand on his wound. The phone falls to the floor beside him as he staggers around, but I don't go for that because I'm more concerned with watching to see what Greg does next.

The answer is him collapsing to the floor by my feet. He begins to ignore the gash in his neck and instead reaches out his hands towards me, as if I am going to be his saviour now. It highlights just how afraid, confused and desperate he is to be seeking help from the person who just inflicted that wound. He must know I have no intention of taking his hand and administering aid.

As the blood continues to drain from him, the realisation that I am willing to watch him die right in front of me dawns on him, and that's when his hands return to his neck, but it's far too late to stem the blood flow now.

Slowly but surely, Greg's breathing becomes more laboured and his movements become less until he is quiet and still.

That's when I realise I have just killed again.

TWENTY-THREE

FERN

I stare at Greg's still body and can't decide whether I want him to move again or not. If he does, it means I am not guilty of murder. Again. But if he doesn't move, it means one very big threat to exposing my secrets has just been eliminated.

In the end, it doesn't matter what I want or don't want because my wishes do not change the fact that Greg stays still. When I carefully feel his neck for a pulse, I do not find one.

He's definitely dead.

There are many things I could do first in this situation. Run from the room and try and put as much distance between myself and this crime scene as possible. Cry out for help so somebody in one of the rooms nearby might hear me and come to offer assistance. Pick up the phone and call reception to tell them they need to request an ambulance to come to this hotel as quickly as possible. Or there is a fourth option: I could forget about doing any of the first three things and, instead, make sure the recording on Greg's phone is deleted before anybody else comes in here and asks what was going on.

So that's what I do. Picking up the phone, which has some of Greg's blood on it, I wipe it away before doing what I wanted to do a few minutes ago. I delete the video and, with it, the evidence Greg had on me.

That should feel like a massive weight has been lifted off my shoulders, but it's not quite as simple as that because there is still the small matter of the dead body to deal with and, despite trying to stay calm, I cannot see how I can talk my way out of this one, but surely it would look less suspicious to at least try then to run away without saying a word. But talking about this is not going to be easy. The first police officer to enter this hotel room is going to ask me to recall the chain of events that led to me stabbing Greg. What am I supposed to say to them? I can't tell them the truth, so I'll need to tell them a lie. But it'll have to be a believable one and, unfortunately, I am struggling to come up with such a thing at this moment in time.

I'm aware this scene will only become even more suspicious the longer I leave notifying someone about it, so I have to think fast. But it's not easy to do that while being in such close proximity to a corpse, so I give myself a brief respite from having to look at Greg's body by going into the bathroom and closing the door behind me. Feeling only a tiny bit better, I lean against the sink and take several deep breaths while wondering if I am going to be sick. It turns out that I'm not, and that means there is nothing else to distract me from having to come up with a plan to get myself out of this. That's when I look up and see my reflection in the mirror and, suddenly, the answer is staring me right in the face.

There is a very clear mark on my left cheek, the place where Greg struck me while we were wrestling shortly before he ran to the door and I stabbed him. He hit me to defend himself but only I know that. What if I tell the police that I was actually the one trying to defend myself and, after he hit me, I was so afraid that I did the only thing I could in the chaos, which was to reach for the bottle and fight back with it?

What if I tell the police that Greg was drunk and after we

got back to our room after the party, he started arguing with me and became violent?

What if I tell them that Greg started this?

Most importantly, what if they believe me?

With Greg dead and his evidence deleted, I would have nothing to worry about then. I'd be seen as the victim, just like I was in Arberness, when the whole village came together to support me in the wake of my husband's murder. Getting away with murder again is a delicious prospect, and if I've done it once before, I don't see why I can't do it again. I know I am strong enough to face police questioning and make it through any interview without giving myself away. I can do this because I've got experience. I can do it again, as many times as I have to.

Steeling myself as I stare at the mark on my face that proves Greg hit me, I run through how this is going to work. In order to pass myself off as the victim, I need to look like the victim and as clear as the mark on my face is, it's not enough. That's why I tear my nightdress in several places to make it look like Greg was pulling at me and trying to drag me to the floor. I still need more though, because this might not be enough to justify stabbing him. I have to make the police believe that I genuinely felt my life was in danger, and the best way to explain why I drew blood from Greg is to show them the blood he drew from me.

Leaving the bathroom, I step over Greg's body, without looking down at it for too long, and walk over to where the shards of glass from the broken bottle lie on the carpet. Picking up the biggest piece I can find, I tell myself to be brave before I use the glass to cut several scratch marks into the palms of my hands: I will say that I got those when I had my hands out in front of myself trying to fend off the bottle.

Satisfied that I look even more like a victim instead of a perpetrator now, I move on to the next part of my plan. What would a woman in my predicament do next, if she had just managed to disarm the man who had been trying to kill her?

She would leave the room and go and find help, of course.

Rushing for the door before I have time to talk myself out of this, I fling it open before falling into the corridor. I'm almost hoping that another guest is out here because it would look very convincing for somebody to see me erupting out of the room covered in blood. But the corridor is quiet, as is to be expected in the middle of the night. However, even though everyone on this floor is sleeping, I plan on waking every single one of them up and, as I start running down the corridor towards the elevators, I bang on as many doors as I can as I pass them while crying out for somebody to help me.

By the time I have made it to the elevator, one guest has emerged from their room. It's a man in his sixties, wearing silk pyjamas, and he looks horrified at his discovery.

'Help me!' I shout before I hit the button that will bring the elevator to this floor, and when he asks me what is wrong, I tell him there is a man in my room trying to kill me. He looks back up the corridor then to where I have just pointed, and is possibly afraid that he is going to see some burly guy coming towards him with a weapon in his hand. I already know the threat has been removed, not that I let on about that, and as the elevator arrives and the doors slide open, I rush inside and hit the button for the ground floor.

I see the man's puzzled face just before the doors close and I start to descend. The few seconds I have in here give me a little time to prepare for my next big act. Then, when the doors open again, I run out screaming into the lobby, and the poor woman behind the reception goes as white as a ghost when she sees me coming towards her.

'Call the police! Please!' I cry as I reach the reception desk and slump against it, getting some of the blood on my hands onto the white marble countertop that separates us.

The receptionist doesn't need telling twice and, as she picks up the phone and calls 999, I start weeping, allowing all the emotion of the night to pour out of me for the receptionist, and any cameras that might be in this lobby that will be checked by a police officer later.

I only stop crying when the first policeman arrives and, by the time more follow, paramedics are on the scene too. A couple come to tend to me and my injuries, but it's the ones who are getting into the elevator that I keep my eye on because it is they who are on their way up to find Greg's body and, when they do, they are going to get confirmation that this hotel is now a major crime scene.

Once that becomes clear, I know it will be time for the questions to start.

I can only hope that I am ready for them.

TWENTY-FOUR

FERN

The cuts on my hands and arms are stinging and the mark on my face has turned into quite the bruise but, fortunately, I am in the best place to have my injuries taken care of. I'm currently sitting on a bed in hospital, where I have been ever since an ambulance brought me here from the hotel that quickly became a very chaotic place once the story of what had happened in Room 6E had emerged.

There were multiple emergency service vehicles in the car park of the hotel as I was led to the vehicle that was to take me away, as well as numerous guests who had come out of their rooms after hearing all the noise and seeing the flashing blue lights outside their windows. All of the people who were standing around in their dressing gowns and pyjamas were gossiping and gawking, and they reminded me of many of the villagers who had done the same back on the day when Drew's body had first been found on the beach in Arberness. There's nothing quite like a good crime to get the general public talking, and I'm sure there are plenty of journalists who have joined the scene now who are also getting in on the act. Fortunately, I was well out of the way before any reporters could show up and stick a microphone in my face, and I am grateful for that. Where I am now is much more private.

Looking around at the pale blue curtains that surround my bed on all sides, I am glad to be by myself and under the care of medical experts. A couple of nurses and a doctor have already examined my injuries and told me that I am going to be okay, something I already knew but had to pretend I was worried about until they said it. But, so far, they haven't actually been able to treat any of my wounds or begin covering them in bandages or plasters. Before that can happen, the police need to document the severity of them.

I've already made it clear to anybody who would listen that I am the victim of physical abuse and, while that has so far helped me avoid having handcuffs wrapped around my wrists in connection with the corpse in my hotel room, it also means I am evidence in a crime. My body is essentially proof of what I have reported and, for the police to consider it, they need to document everything that has happened to me.

That's why I'm waiting for somebody to come and take photos of my hands.

I understand why the images have to be captured, I just hope that it will not go as far as those images being shown to a jury in court. If it does then it means I have gone to trial for Greg's murder, and that would suggest that I've not done a very good job of convincing the police of my story. I'm not planning on having it come to that but, unfortunately, it's not up to me. It's up to the investigating officers to decide whether they believe me or not and, as two of them pull back the curtain and enter, along with a woman holding a camera, I prepare to keep up my act.

Doing my best to look anxious and afraid as I hold out my hands and allow my injuries to be documented, I also make sure to enquire about the current condition of the man who caused these injuries.

'Where is Roger? Is he here?' I ask the two officers, making sure when I do to use the fake name I was given and not the real name I know the dead man actually went by.

The two officers share a grim look before telling me that somebody will be with me soon to talk about what has happened and then, with the photos taken, all three of them leave. That's when the nurses are allowed back in and, finally, my wounds are covered in bandages, and I don't have to look at all the damage I did to myself any more. Only when that is done do I get to meet the detective heading up the investigation into what happened in that hotel room. When they enter, I see a smiling woman in her thirties who doesn't look old enough or beaten down enough to hold such a lofty position in the police. She is a far cry from Detective Tomlin, the detective I encountered in Arberness with his ill-fitting suits and haggard expression. This detective looks keener than him, certainly much fresher, and while her suit is smarter than any I ever saw Tomlin wearing, I can only hope that her smarts in solving this case are just as lacking as his ultimately were.

'I'm Detective Bell and this is PC Green,' she says, referring to the officer who has entered behind her. 'I'm just going to ask you a few questions and we are going to record them. Is that okay?'

I stare at the tape recorder in the officer's hands before nodding my head.

'Can you state your name for the tape, please.'

'Fern Devlin.'

'How are you feeling?'

The detective's first couple of questions are easy ones to answer, but I make sure to stay on my guard because I doubt she will go this softly on me for the whole time we are together.

'I'm okay,' I mumble before I have a question of my own for her.

'Where is Roger? Nobody will tell me what is going on with him,' I say.

There is an awkward pause then, before Bell gives me the 'sad' news.

'The man you were with in the hotel room has passed away,' she says, and I make sure to look shocked at first, before I start crying a few seconds after that.

After I've been offered a handkerchief to wipe my tears, I stifle some sobs before asking if I am in trouble for hurting him.

'Why don't you talk me through what happened,' Bell says as she takes a seat on the edge of my bed, and I notice her eyes inspecting my bandages.

'I don't know. It all happened so fast,' I begin with, though I know I'll have to go into a lot more detail than that before the detective leaves me alone.

'Just take your time and if you want to do this a little later then I understand. But it would be very helpful to us if we could just get some idea of what happened in that room as soon as possible.'

I nod my head to show that I understand that she is just doing her job, and then I do mine, beginning my latest charade that will, I hope, see me avoid prison once again.

'It was my fortieth birthday yesterday and Roger threw me a surprise party.'

'Roger?'

'Yes,' I reply, thinking it's good that the detective keeps looking puzzled as to why I used the wrong name for him.

'What was your relationship with him?'

'He was my boyfriend. We met a few months ago.'

'How did you meet?'

'In a bar. We just got chatting.'

It sounds so innocent when I put it like that but, sadly, it was anything but.

'Okay, so what happened during the party?' the detective

asks me before glancing at her colleague to make sure he is paying attention too.

'Nothing, the party was great. I enjoyed myself and I thought Roger did too. But then we went upstairs to the room he had booked for us both and that's when I realised he wasn't happy at all.'

'Why not?'

'He said he didn't like some of my friends. He felt they were judging him because he was just a salesman and my ex-husband used to be a doctor.'

'And your ex-husband's name is?'

'Drew. Drew Devlin.'

I'm sure the detective must recognise that name, but, if she does, she doesn't let on. Instead, she just invites me to keep going.

'I told him my friends all liked him and that he was just reading too much into it. But he'd had quite a bit to drink and even though I told him to get into bed, he was too fired up to relax. He kept pacing around and wouldn't settle.'

'How much had he had to drink?'

'I don't know. It was a party. A lot, I imagine. We did shots. He had several beers. He was drunk, just like everybody else was.'

'And what was he like when he was under the influence of alcohol?'

'He was usually okay. But this time was different.'

I lower my head then as if mentally recalling how different that time really was, and, by breaking eye contact with the detective, I buy myself a little time to think about the answer to her next question.

'Different how?'

'He was frustrated,' I say, only looking up again when I feel a satisfactory amount of time has passed. 'He started getting angry. I'd never seen him like that. I started to worry.'

'Why were you worried?'

'He wouldn't settle down and I knew he'd had a lot to drink. Then he shouted at me.'

'Why?'

'Because I was telling him to get into bed, but he wouldn't listen to me. He told me to shut up and then when I went to take his hand and help him into bed, he hit me.'

I gesture to the bruise on my face, and Bell describes what I have just done for the record.

'Then what happened?' she asks me as I silently remind myself to stay strong because I only have to do this once and it will be over soon.

'I was stunned. I guess I was in shock. I started to cry and ask Roger why he had just hurt me.'

'And what did he say?'

'He said it was because I was annoying him.'

'Had he ever done anything like that before?'

I shake my head but it's not the only thing shaking. My hands are unsteady too. I guess it's nerves and adrenaline from being in a situation like this one, but, to the detective, it must just look like I'm struggling with flashbacks and bad memories, so I don't need to try and calm myself down too quickly.

'No, it was the first time. But once was enough, and I knew I wanted to get away from him then in case he tried to hit me again, so I went to put on some more clothes because I wanted to leave the room.'

'And what did he do?'

'He tried to stop me. Told me I couldn't go anywhere. That I had to stay there with him. Then, when I wouldn't listen, he broke his beer bottle and came at me with the broken edge.'

It's a tall tale, but I make sure to really sell it by forcing out some more tears, and the detective allows me a few moments to compose myself before I go on.

'I put my hands up to defend myself but he kept jabbing the

bottle at me. It cut my hands and I cried out with pain but he wouldn't stop,' I say, doing my best to look traumatised as I speak.

'Then what happened?' the detective asks, and she looks like she'd rather be asking me anything but, because she can see how uncomfortable I am at being made to recall the sequence of events.

'I thought I was going to die,' I say, really selling it now. 'I thought he would kill me if I didn't fight back, so I dodged the bottle when he lunged at me and then I was able to knock it out of his hand. He dived on the floor for it, but I went for it too and we both wrestled as we tried to get to it. I managed to pick it up first and when I did, I just hit him with it to try and get him to stay back.'

'You hit him with it. Where exactly?'

'I didn't know at first. It was all a blur. I think I got him in his neck.'

'You hit him with the bottle, or you stabbed him with it?'

'I don't know. I was just trying to get him to stop. You have to believe me! I thought he was going to kill me!'

I break down then, allowing all my tears out, but also making sure to hold up my hands so both the detective and the officer behind her can clearly see all my bandages – because they're a very important part of my story.

Only when I have quietened again does Detective Bell dare voice another question.

'What did you do after you stabbed him?'

'I dropped the bottle and ran for the door. I just wanted to get out of there.'

'You didn't wait to see if he was okay?'

'No, I was scared he'd get up and then I thought he'd try and hurt me.'

That's my story and I'm sticking to it, and Detective Bell sees that I have nothing more to add in terms of what happened in that room before she and her colleagues got there. Before our interview is over, she has something else to mention, though this relates to a different matter than me stabbing my boyfriend.

'You said his name was Roger,' she says, and I nod my head.

'Yes. Why?'

'My colleagues checked the ID in his wallet and we believe his name was actually Greg.'

'What?' I gasp, making sure to look appropriately surprised.

'You didn't know?'

'No, he told me he was called Roger! Why would he lie to me? And why would he lie to all my family and friends too? We all knew him as Roger! Why was he using a fake name?'

'We're not sure yet, but we're looking into it.'

'Wait, isn't what he did a crime? Who was he? Was he married? Was I his mistress?' I cry, warming easily to my theme. 'Is that why he gave me a fake name? What other lies did he tell me?'

I'm throwing out all sorts of fake theories and ideas, as well as highlighting the fact that Greg broke the law by lying to me at the start of our relationship, because the more I do that, the more I can muddy the waters and bring the deceased's credibility into question. I need the police to see Greg as a violent, drunken liar and me as his poor victim, who fell for his lies and almost lost her life by being with him.

But has it worked?

For now, it appears so, because Detective Bell and Officer Green leave me alone to continue my recovery on the bed. As I lie back and listen to the sounds of the busy hospital on the other side of my curtains, I think that actually went quite well.

I daren't say it out loud in case anyone overhears me, or I jinx it, but I'm certainly thinking it now.

I'm thinking I've just gotten away with murder again...

PART TWO

WHEN THE POLICE CAME

TWENTY-FIVE

TOMLIN

I don't have to look at the time on my alarm clock as I wearily reach for it and turn it off. I already know it's 6 a.m. because that's the time the alarm goes off every day during the week, and sometimes on the weekend too if my job requires it. I also don't need to spend too long thinking about how long I have been in my bed. I know it's usually well after midnight before I slump onto my mattress and close my eyes and last night was no different.

As always when a new day dawns, I feel exhausted and like I still haven't recovered from the previous one. And, as always, I am forcing myself to get up to do it all again, solely for two things. The first is money, the likes of which a lifetime of this type of work will still never give me enough of. The second is for justice, or at least that's what I try to remind myself when things get particularly tough and I wonder why on earth I ever wanted to become a detective.

There's no doubt I have gone down a tough career path, one that barely allows me time for myself let alone other people, which might explain why I am waking up without anyone else in this bed beside me, nor hearing the voices of any little children filtering through from another room. A pessimistic person could say that I am married to my job, but if I am then it is an unhappy marriage. I'm worn out and spend half my time wondering why I still bother to do what I do. Sure, I get to help catch criminals every now and again, but even doing that just makes me aware of how many bad people there are in the world, and the lengths many of them are prepared to go to in order to get whatever it is they want. It's hardly the best way to see the good in things when you're constantly having to investigate the bad. However, it is what I am paid to do. So I better get out of this bed and keep doing it if I want to continue paying the mortgage on this two-bedroom home of mine that contains several frozen meals in the freezer, a big TV I never get time to watch and a sofa I never get time to sit on, and, last but not least, a wardrobe full of my bad suits.

I know they are bad suits because they were so cheap when I bought them. If that wasn't enough to confirm it, several of my colleagues have teased me about my fashion choices at work, saying that I look like I lost a bet or tell me I'm dressed like their late great-grandfather. Whatever. I don't dress to win any fashion awards or impress anybody. I have to wear a suit so I do, but nobody told me it had to be an expensive one.

Forcing myself out of bed and over to my wardrobe, I pick out a suit that I've had for a few years now and lay it down on the bed before preparing to go and get in the shower. Just before I do, I check my phone. It's lying on the carpet in the corner of my bedroom connected to the charging cable; the reason it's all the way down there, and not on my bedside table where it would be more accessible, is because the damn cable doesn't reach that far. I wasn't blessed with great plug socket choices in this house, just like the north of England where I reside is not blessed with great weather.

As I listen to the wind and rain hitting my window, sounds that are making me reluctant to pull open the curtains and look outside, I pick up my phone and check for any missed calls or messages. I keep my phone on loud in case there are any urgent calls in the middle of the night regarding one of the cases I am working on, though even then I have been known to occasionally sleep through any notifications. Sometimes, no matter what, exhaustion overrides a loud ringtone. In today's case, I have no missed calls, though I do have one message waiting for me. It's from a number I don't recognise, and it was sent in the early hours of the morning, which immediately has me assuming it must be some kind of spam message sent out from a sales number. I feel even less confident about it being genuine when I read the message on my screen.

I'm at the PinkTree Hotel in Manchester. Just in case something happens to me, you need to hear this.

Frowning, thinking this is probably a prank from one of my colleagues, I open the message. There is a video attachment with it. Preparing myself for it to be one big joke once I start the video, I go ahead and hit the play button to get it over with. But I see a black screen. At first, I'm not sure what I am supposed to be looking at, and then I realise it's not what I can see but what I can hear that matters.

I can hear a woman's voice and, as I listen to it, I feel as if I recognise it from somewhere. But where? Then I hear a man speaking and I recognise his voice too, though again I can't quite place it. I can't place it until I hear the names *Drew* and *Alice* mentioned, as well as a reference to the village of *Arberness* and that's when I figure out who these people are. The woman is Fern Devlin, Drew's widow and someone whom I spoke to on multiple occasions during the investigation into her husband's murder. And the man is Greg, the guy who accosted me the other day in the car park of the police station and took me for a pint, to tell me he had a wild theory about the real truth behind what had happened in that sleepy village earlier in the year.

As I listen to the recording, I hear all sorts of interesting things, not least of which is Fern admitting she knew about Drew's affair before his death, which is not something she told me when I questioned her. From what I recall, she was shocked to learn of his affair, a fact that quite quickly garnered her sympathy from me and my colleagues and made her seem less like a suspect and more of a victim. And our sympathy for her only grew when all the evidence pointed to Drew's lover – Alice. Although right now I am hearing that Fern made sure she got her revenge on Alice as well as Drew. And what is this about Rory, Alice's husband, who wound up dead shortly afterwards? According to Fern in this recording, he didn't kill himself like we all believed. Instead, she is saying that he was a problem for her, who had to be dealt with.

I realise then as I stand in my untidy bedroom and listen to the rain outside that it seems Greg was right. Not only that but he has also been able to get what he told me he was going to try and obtain.

He has genuine evidence relating to Fern and her crimes.

I realise I need to call Greg and have him corroborate what he has sent me, so I ring his number and wait for him to answer. The call never connects and, even after three more times of trying, there is no answer from him. That's frustrating, but it is still early so maybe he isn't being woken up by his phone like I am sometimes not woken by mine. No bother. I will speak to him soon enough, just like I will be speaking to Fern too.

Suddenly feeling very awake, I decide to forgo my usual morning shower and cup of coffee and just get dressed as quickly as I can so I can leave promptly. I want to take this recording straight to one of my superiors and have them listen to it. Some detectives might be wary of producing new evidence that could potentially sec a previously closed case get reopened, especially when they were the ones who were originally commended for solving it so efficiently in the first place, but not me. I just want the right thing to be done, and if the wrong thing has been done previously then it needs to be corrected as quickly as possible.

Not liking the idea of contributing to the incarceration of a possible innocent woman like Alice, I try not to dwell too much on that until a little further down the line, as I reach my car and jump in. Starting the engine, I reverse off my driveway as my radio automatically turns on and, when it does, I get the morning update from the national news.

As the reporter talks about issues in Westminster before moving on to a very minor earthquake that was recorded in south Wales overnight, there is nothing on here to concern me as I drive through the rain-soaked streets towards the station. But then I hear something that changes all that: the reporter mentions the PinkTree Hotel in Manchester, and I remember that was where Greg said he was last night when he sent me his message. It's the next part that really gets my attention though: a man's body was discovered in one of the rooms of that hotel in the early hours of the morning and, at present, the only witness to what might have happened is the unnamed woman he was sharing that room with.

Hitting the brakes and pulling over quickly to the side of the road, I feel a knot in my stomach as I wonder if this was why Greg wasn't answering his phone earlier.

Is he the dead man in the hotel room?

If so, that must mean Fern was the woman who was with him.

If that's the case, has she already struck again?

TWENTY-SIX

FERN

It's not easy to do simple tasks like boil a kettle or butter a slice of toast with my hands bandaged and still healing, but that's why I have accepted the offer of help from my best friend. As I sit on the sofa and recuperate, Claire is the one who is in the kitchen making me cups of tea and serving me snacks. I make sure to keep thanking her for all she is doing to help me.

'It's no problem. None at all,' she says for what must be the seventh time since she arrived at my house, not long after I had got back from the hospital. I know she doesn't want me to feel guilty about needing her assistance. I also know she feels sorry for me after what seems like another huge slice of bad luck with the opposite sex, so she can't do enough for me at present. When she's not running back and forth from the kitchen with cups and plates then she is plumping up cushions, passing me the remote control for the TV or offering to get the hoover out – it's all very kind of her.

If only she knew I wasn't the damsel in distress that she thinks I am.

I was discharged from the hospital this morning after the staff there were satisfied that my wounds were healing well enough for me to finish my recovery at home. I was also allowed to go straight to my house without having to go via the police station first, after the detective looking into what happened with Greg told me she is satisfied with my version of events. She says she might have more questions for me at some point but they should just be a formality – I appear to be in the clear again.

I'm not getting ahead of myself and allowing myself to feel too smug, though; but it is difficult to not start thinking that I have a talent for this kind of thing. How many times can a woman like me fool everyone before they realise what I've really done? The answer might be forever and, if it is, then I will gladly take that.

'Another drink? What about a sandwich?' Claire offers as she walks back into the lounge and picks up my latest empty cup and plate.

'No, I'm fine, thanks,' I say, but Claire studies me as if she thinks I am lying. I suppose from her point of view, I must be because how could a woman in my position actually be fine? As she sees it, I have gone from celebrating my fortieth birthday with my new boyfriend to almost losing my life at his hands just a few hours later. Now he is dead while I am covered in cuts and bruises. It's been quite the turnaround since I last saw my friend when we were both standing at a bar and toasting to the second half of my life.

'Are you sure?' Claire goes on, not taking the hint that I'd prefer it if she stopped fussing over me. 'I could go to the supermarket and get you some bits there. The fridge is looking a little bare. How about I go and do a big shop for you? You don't need to make a list, I'll just get the essentials and anything I see that you might like. Chocolates. Magazines. A bottle of wine. Don't worry about giving me any money, it's my treat.'

Claire looks like she is ready to rush out the door and drive to the supermarket for me right now, but I don't need her to. I'm exhausted just watching her so that's why I tell her that the best thing she could do for me right now is take a seat beside me on the sofa, slow down a little bit and just have a chat with me.

'Oh, okay,' Claire says when I ask her to sit down. She does as I ask but she appears a little awkward, and that's when I realise that all her running around for me was most likely because that is an easier thing to do than stop and have a difficult conversation with me about what has just happened.

I get it. She feels guilty about what happened to me in that hotel room, or at least what she thinks happened to me, because she helped arrange the surprise party with Greg, or Roger as we all knew him before. I'm sure she thinks that if she had maybe asked him a few more questions or just not helped him arrange the party at the hotel at all then none of this would have happened. But this is not her fault, and she mustn't blame herself, which is what I start to make clear to her.

'He had us all fooled,' I say to Claire once she has finally stayed still long enough for me to get my point across. 'If I didn't know who he really was then there was no way you were going to know, was there? So don't feel bad for falling for his lies too. He was good at it and the main thing is that I'm okay.'

Claire's eyes suddenly well up with tears; it's as if my admission that she is not to carry any of the blame for what happened has unburdened her all at once. I guess she never would have forgiven herself if I had died in that hotel room, and would have always regretted replying to Greg's messages and saying yes to the party. But there was no danger of me ever being the one who died there, although she can't know that much.

'It's not just that,' she says to me quietly after she has picked up the box of tissues from my coffee table and dabbed her eyes. 'It's everything. It's all that has happened to you. It's just so unfair.'

I see then that Claire is not just upset about her role in what transpired, but with the overall sense of injustice that she believes I have suffered in my life.

'First Drew and now this,' she goes on, looking at me as if she cannot fathom how I am still able to function after such a bad sequence of events. 'You don't deserve any of this. You deserve to be happy. I want you to be happy.'

'Hey, listen. I'm okay,' I say, taking Claire's hand and trying to prove to her that I am a lot tougher than she thinks I am. 'Don't feel sorry for me. Those men are the ones who did things wrong, not me. I'm still here so that's all that matters, okay?'

Claire nods and gives my hand a squeeze before I make a joke about my next partner and what the odds are of him being a serial killer or something as equally dramatic as that. That helps lighten the mood, and once Claire has composed herself she goes back to doing what she seems to do best, which is fussing over me. I agree to her making me another cup of tea, if only to have a brief break from having to keep acting in front of her. As she leaves the room, I can relax a little more. But only a little because I still have plenty on my mind after all that has happened.

Greg might be dead and the evidence he obtained deleted, but that doesn't necessarily mean this is over. That's because I know he visited Alice in prison.

The only thing I don't know is what they talked about.

It had to have been about me, and I presume they were united in their belief that I am the one who framed Alice for Drew's murder. I also wonder if they were on the right track to finding out what I did to Rory too. Because of that, even with Greg out of the picture, Alice is still a threat. Once she hears about Greg's demise, there is nothing to stop her spouting off all her theories to any police officer that will listen. That's not to say that any of them will believe her, but there is something powerful about a pretty woman trying to get men to be on her side, and I know all too well just how strong Alice's powers of persuasion are. She made Drew do some crazy things while they were together, and she also motivated Greg to do something as foolish as fake a relationship with me, to try and get her out of prison, so who is to say what might happen next?

The last thing I need is her getting somebody on her side who actually has the power to do something about all this. Somebody like Tomlin, a detective who, instead of playing games and trying to trick me into making a mistake, simply relies on solid, old-fashioned police tactics to catch me out. I don't want to be taken back into an interview room and questioned over and over again about what happened with Drew, Rory or Greg. I certainly don't wish for the media to start thinking there is more to my story, and for them to flood the news channels with theories about me actually being a criminal mastermind who kills men and gets away with it.

If that happened, they'd stop calling me the doctor's widow and start calling me the Black Widow.

Therefore, it is imperative that Alice stays quiet and isn't able to get somebody else to pick up where Greg left off. If not, this will never be over, and I'll never be able to trust another person in my life again. They all might be on Alice's side rather than mine.

But how do I silence a woman who is determined to keep talking until she is out of prison and I am put in her place?

I need to go and talk to her myself.

I wonder if I could request a visit with her. I could do it under the guise of needing to see her to seek closure after what she did to my husband. The prison authorities should buy that excuse and while Alice surely won't, she might accept my request, thinking it will give her the chance to at least see me face to face and say to me whatever she wants to say.

I'm sure she has plenty she wants to get off her chest, as do I, so how about it?

One of two things could happen during our meeting. Either

I find out that Alice has another ace up her sleeve in trying to bring me down and, if so, I can be prepared for that. Or I discover that Greg really was her only hope. At that point, I can revel in her misfortune and tell her that no matter what she does and how many people she tries to convince to believe her, I will never ever make a mistake that might let her be released.

It will be a delicious moment to sit across a table from her, look into her eyes and tell her that she had one shot at catching me and she blew it. Then, after reminding her that all of this only happened because she started an affair with my husband, I will walk out of that visiting room and not look back, leaving Alice to languish in that place for many more years to come.

I'm so eager now that I decide I will put in my request for a visit as soon as Claire has left me alone. Then I will just have to wait patiently and hope that Alice accepts it.

Surely she will and I'm so confident that I am going to find myself a hotel to stay at in Carlisle so I can be close to the prison, meaning I'll be ready to go just as soon as Alice agrees to meet with me. As a reason for leaving Manchester shortly, I'll just tell my family and friends that I've booked myself into a spa in the countryside for a few days to recuperate after recent events. They'll believe that and it'll give me a reason to be away for a while. But really, all I will be doing is waiting to get the green light to walk into Carlisle prison and see my old foe.

I know it's going to happen.

Alice will agree to see me.

It's a chance for her to meet with the woman she believes framed her for murder.

How could she refuse an opportunity like that?

TWENTY-SEVEN

TOMLIN

As far as I'm concerned, I was wrong and nothing proves that more than the fact that the man who came to me with his theories and his concerns for his own wellbeing was found dead in the early hours of this morning.

I messed up Drew Devlin's murder case and, because of that, an innocent woman went to prison and her innocent saviour has wound up in an even worse place: the mortuary.

The thing about me is that I'm not afraid to admit my mistakes, which is why I've spent hours persuading my superiors that we should arrest Fern Devlin and bring her in for questioning so she can answer to the things she has said in that recording. This whole thing might not reflect well on me. It may not enhance my future career prospects – nobody wants to be the detective who got it wrong and had to rely on a member of the public to fix it for them – but the most important thing is that things are sorted out sooner rather than later: Alice Richardson deserves that.

After hearing that recording, I was convinced Alice was innocent. She has suffered a wrongful conviction, but I also heard she had been assaulted while in custody, and that only makes me feel even more guilty for messing up the investigation. At least she is okay, as far as I know and, hopefully, there won't be any long-lasting damage to her, either physically or mentally, when she does get out. She might sue somebody for what she's been through, but that's a matter for another day. Right now, the focus is firmly on making sure the right person takes her place in that prison cell.

It wasn't easy to get the people who needed to listen to that recording I received from Greg to listen to me. It's a fact that nobody in the police force likes to go over old cases when there are so many new ones waiting to be solved. But after hearing that Greg had died not long after he had sent me that evidence, I was not going to let his sacrifice be in vain. I cannot believe that Fern not only killed Greg but was also about to get away with murder again. As far as I know, she was released from the hospital and went straight home rather than straight into police custody.

I've been told the story she gave to the detective in Manchester was a plausible one. She has claimed Greg attacked her, and she killed him in self-defence. Perhaps that would have been easier to believe without anything else to consider, but armed with a recording from the deceased – who already seemed to be aware that harm might come his way soon – I was easily able to cast doubt on Fern's story.

That's why I am currently in a car on my way to Fern's place of residence now.

I'm travelling in a convoy with several other force vehicles, all of them filled with police officers. When we get to our destination, we have a warrant to search Fern's property as well as bring her in for questioning. It does not look good for Fern. I am more than ready to put that woman in handcuffs and find out exactly what she has done. There is no doubt it will be a very different type of conversation to the ones I had with her in Arberness. Then, I thought she was grieving the loss of her partner. I expect I'll be much more forceful with my line of questioning this time, and I imagine I'll have to bite my tongue a couple of times to stop losing my temper if she persists with her lies. That's because I could easily take out my frustration on her; after all, she already fooled me once and, thanks to her, I'm sure I'll have some questions of my own to answer when this is all over and done with. But for now, she is the one in the spotlight, and as I arrive in Manchester, I am just itching to see the surprised look on her face when she opens her front door to me standing on her doorstep.

I imagine I'll be quite the blast from the past.

The skies are grey, and it's looking like there is a storm on the way, as we head towards the address we have after consulting with our colleagues in the Manchester police. If only Fern knew what storm was really coming then I doubt she would be feeling quite as comfortable as she surely is at the moment. She must think she is so clever sitting at home and revelling in all the sympathy she is getting for losing not just one partner but two. Arriving on her street, I see just how nice the place she calls home is. These properties must cost a small fortune, certainly far more than anything I could afford, which only serves to draw my ire. While I've spent my life trying to do the right thing, Fern has broken several laws and been rewarded with a lifestyle like this one. That lifestyle is over now, and where she is going her neighbours will be very different to the ones she has around here.

This place is a far cry from where poor Greg lived and I know that because I have read the report from the team of officers who conducted a search of his home after his death. Having gone to his address to see if there was anything there that might have helped them form a better understanding of the deceased, they had discovered the victim was not exactly living an opulent life before he passed. But they also discovered he was leading a very focused one, because there was a very interesting wallchart discovered in his home, one that clearly showed he was a man on a mission. All the photos of Fern and Alice that were there, not to mention the numerous newspaper articles about Drew's death, painted a picture of a man who was clearly not only fascinated with the case of the doctor's death but also convinced there was more to it. That discovery only added further weight to the idea that Greg was trying to expose Fern, giving her reason to want to shut him up any way she could.

As the car comes to a stop, I get out quickly and pace up the driveway, getting closer by the second to the impressive property. If this house was paid for by Drew Devlin's life insurance policy, which I suspect it was, it will soon be considered proceeds of crime and Fern will forfeit ownership of all of it. That'll be the least of her problems though. Reaching her front door, I make sure to knock swiftly and loudly, overeager to see the reaction on the homeowner's face.

But the door doesn't open, so I knock again. And again. Still no answer.

No bother. All I need to do now is stand aside and let my colleagues take it from here.

Sure enough, they do just that and, as the door is kicked in and the police make their presence known verbally, I allow several officers to stream inside before I follow them in.

As I take in the spacious hallway, my colleagues spread out and search each room, all of them wondering if they are going to be the first to find the homeowner and bring her to me. However, the longer they search, the more I start to worry that Fern isn't home. Once the upstairs has been checked just as thoroughly as the downstairs, I get confirmation.

'There's no one here, guv,' a disappointed PC tells me, and I nod to confirm I understand before I step back outside and look up and down the street.

'I guess we'll just wait for her to get back then,' I say, more than happy to wait for as long as it takes to arrest Fern. If it has to be when she comes back from whatever errand she has been running then so be it.

Unfortunately, the wait goes on and on and, after a couple of hours pass, I am starting to fear that Fern has somehow figured out that we were on to her and has made a run for it before we got here. Terrified that I might have failed yet again when it comes to this woman, I'm steeling myself to make a call to my superiors to give them more bad news, when I receive a call of my own. It's from a colleague in Carlisle and they have some very interesting information to pass on to me.

'Fern Devlin has put in a visitor request to see Alice Richardson,' I am told.

'She's done what?' I ask, seeking clarification. I'm surprised that Fern would have the audacity to do such a thing. The information is repeated to me and now I know what her intentions are, I have an idea.

'Approve that request and set up the visit as quickly as you can,' I instruct the man at the other end of the line. 'If we know where Fern is going to be then we can arrest her, so the sooner you approve that request then the sooner we can have her in custody. If it can't be today then tomorrow at the latest.'

My order is understood and, as I end the call, I tell those standing around outside this house with me that there has been a change of plan and we'll most likely have to wait until tomorrow to make our arrest. I'm as frustrated at the delay as everybody else, but on the off-chance we can get lucky today, I ask for an unmarked car with an undercover police officer in it to stay on this street and keep watch on Fern's house, just in case she comes back at any point today. She might do but, if not, it's no big deal —we'll just get her tomorrow. Even though it seems like we have had a wasted journey today, she might end up saving us a lot of time in the long run.

That's because she'll already be in prison when we arrest her tomorrow.

TWENTY-EIGHT

FERN

My drive north to Carlisle was relatively easy, barring the one section of the motorway that was undergoing road works. But even a twenty-minute delay to my journey like that one couldn't deter me from getting to where I needed to be. I also had good news when I reached my destination, because the notification in my inbox told me that my visitation request had been approved and an appointment had been set up.

I presumed I'd have to spend a few days up here waiting for my chance, but it was even quicker than I assumed.

I'm going to get to see Alice tomorrow.

With only a short journey to make to the prison now that I've already got the bulk of the driving out of the way, I've checked myself in to the nicest hotel I could find in the area, and from my room's window I have a lovely view of the rolling green hills that surround this northerly UK city. I'm in my room now, lying on my bed and watching TV, with a load of snacks sitting on the duvet beside me, and I'm content to stay this way until I go to sleep.

Despite the injuries to my hands, I managed the drive easily enough, just like I'm managing to change the channel and pick up my glass of water. I didn't need Claire's help quite as much as she thought I did earlier. Bless my friend, she even offered to sleep over at my house to keep an eye on me and offer further assistance, but I told her that wasn't necessary and it most certainly wasn't, just like I didn't need my parents or any of my other friends coming to my aid either. I'm a big girl and I can handle a few cuts and bruises, and I've proven it by getting myself here without anybody's assistance.

I will also prove it tomorrow when I walk into that prison and take my seat opposite Alice.

It's going to be the first time I have seen her in the flesh since she was led out of that courtroom after being found guilty of Drew's murder. I'm very much looking forward to it. It's a shame I won't be looking my best when I do see her, what with the bruise still on my face and my hands still wrapped in bandages, but that's just the way it is. I can't help that I had to do what I did just to keep my freedom, but it's done now and while these wounds will heal and soon be forgotten, the necessity of what I did in that hotel room will endure.

It's much nicer to be in a hotel room that isn't filled with broken glass, incriminating videos and a male corpse. I am enjoying the serenity here as I stuff a few more chocolates into my mouth and lie back on my pillow. But my peace is disturbed a moment later when I hear my phone bleep and, when I pick it up, I see I have a text message from my new neighbour in Manchester, Rosa.

Rosa lives next door to the house I have just purchased, and I have chatted with her briefly on a couple of occasions in the short time I have been living there. She told me she has lived in the area for over thirty years and that it has changed a lot since then. In return, I told her I was very much looking forward to being a part of the neighbourhood and she should let me know if she ever needed me to help her with anything. It's always important to get along with the neighbours. I saw my politeness had been rewarded when Rosa asked for my phone number so she could invite me whenever she hosted barbeques in the summer, or wine and cheese evenings in the winter. I wasn't exactly desperate to spend numerous evenings with her and several of the other people on my street, but I had given her my number just to be nice, figuring I could easily make up an excuse to get out of whatever party she was organising in future if I needed to. Now I see she has messaged me, and my first thought is that the invitations have already begun. But I'm wrong.

She's not inviting me to a party at her place.

She is simply asking if I am OK.

I'm not sure why she is asking me such a thing, but I figure she must just be checking in with me to see how I am getting on in my new home. Or maybe she has seen me leaving the house with my bandaged hands and bruised face and is worried that I had an accident. She might even have called around just now to check on me only to find I'm not answering the door, hence her message. Whatever it is, I better be polite and reply to let her know that I am fine, so I compose a message back to her telling her that I am well and asking her how she is. I expect I'll get a fairly standard reply in which she tells me she is okay too and then the conversation will probably peter out quite quickly from there. But that is not what happens at all. That's because Rosa's next message has me sitting upright on the bed and staring at my phone in horror.

I'm just asking because I saw the police at your house earlier. There were a lot of them, and they went inside, even though you weren't home because your car wasn't on the drive. Did you know about that?

The fact that my whole body is suddenly gripped with fear would tell Rosa that I absolutely did not know about that if she was here to see me now. But she isn't, thankfully, and I am alone as I try to process this very frightening information.

The police were not only at my house but went in my house? For them to have gone in without me being there must mean they had a warrant to search the place and, if that's the case, they must have reason to suspect me of a crime.

But how can they?

And which crime is it that they suspect me of exactly?

I've no idea if they are looking for me in connection with Drew's and Rory's deaths or Greg's more recent one, but either way, it is not good news. I've been careful. I've covered my tracks. Or at least I thought I had. What if I'm wrong? What if I have slipped up somewhere, made a mistake, failed to tie up a loose end? Then I would be screwed. But I haven't done that. If I had messed up then the police would have arrested me sooner, wouldn't they? I wouldn't have got away with things for so long.

I have so many questions, as does Rosa, who I ignore for the time being because replying to her is the least of my worries at present. The problem is the questions I have are the kind that only the police can answer for me. But I'm hardly going to go and ask them, am I?

By the sounds of it, I now have to do everything I can to stay away from them.

Can I manage it?

And what does this mean for my meeting with Alice tomorrow?

TWENTY-NINE

ALICE

There haven't been many things I've looked forward to since I came to prison, but I have something in my schedule that I'm counting down to now. It's my visit from Fern, and while it was a big shock to find out she had requested to see me, there was no way I was going to turn down the chance to meet her again.

Needless to say, I have a lot of things to talk about with her and I imagine she has the same with me, so the conversation shouldn't be dull, that's for sure. There is a big part of me wondering why she would take such a risk as to come here and see me when she could easily just leave me alone for the rest of my sentence. There must be something she specifically wants to get from our meeting, and I can't help but think it must be to do more than gloat.

Is she worried that I am on to her and wants to know exactly what I am doing about it?

If that's the case, maybe I could be the one to gloat. It sure would be sweet if I got to turn the tables on her and make her worry about her life being ruined after she has so successfully ruined mine.

I'm not going to know for sure until I actually see her, but visiting time is fast approaching, so I don't have long to wait. For the time being, I am sitting patiently in my cell and waiting for the door to be unlocked by one of the wardens who will lead me to that visiting room where all will be revealed. As I wait, I wish that Greg was coming to see me too today. I'd love to hear from him again and find out how his progress is going. He hasn't written to me or requested another visit since our last one and, while I don't expect him to be in touch with me daily, it would be good to know if he is getting any closer to uncovering the truth. I'd also be lying if I said I didn't find him quite handsome, or maybe it's the fact he is the only person in the world who seems to be trying to help me. Whatever it is, I hope my next visit will be from him.

It's a shame the bruises on my face haven't healed before Fern sees me. I am still carrying some of the evidence of Kelly's attack on me, and while my stay in hospital was short, I wouldn't say I'm back to feeling one hundred per cent yet. My body is feeling stiff and swollen and the anxiety sickness I was feeling even before Kelly assaulted me has gone up a notch. These days, feeling nauseous is just as much a part of my daily routine as meal times or lights out.

I have a welcome distraction from my worries when I hear footsteps outside my cell, so I stand up to show that I am ready to go when I'm told to. But as the door opens, it's not just a familiar warden I see. There's another man too and it's someone I recognise. It's the detective who questioned me after my arrest and ultimately supported the evidence that had me sentenced for Drew's murder.

What is Tomlin doing here?

I stare at him as he enters my cell and don't say anything in reply when he rather sheepishly offers me a greeting.

'What's happening?' are the first words out of my mouth after the warden has left us to talk in private. There is a brief moment when I can't help but fantasise that I'm just about to be told the misunderstanding has been cleared up and now I am free to leave. Sadly, that is not what happens at all.

'I believe you have been corresponding with a Greg Atkins,' Detective Tomlin says, and I nod my head. 'Perhaps you'd like to sit down.'

Such a suggestion is never followed by good news, so I stay standing and ask what is going on with Greg. Then I hear it and I wish I hadn't bothered.

'I'm afraid Greg passed away in the early hours of yesterday morning,' Tomlin tells me.

As my brain tries to quickly process that shocking information, I put my hands to my mouth and gasp. 'What happened?'

'He was stabbed in the neck with a broken beer bottle,' comes the very grim reply.

'What? Who stabbed him?'

Tomlin doesn't say anything for a moment, and it is as if he is giving me the chance to figure out the answer to that question myself. Unfortunately, I do.

'Fern,' I gasp, and Tomlin solemnly nods his head.

'She's evil! That bitch is the one who is behind all of this! She killed Drew or she got Rory to do it for her and then she killed him! I've been framed!' I cry, unleashing all my woes on the detective who didn't believe my protestations of innocence when he arrested me in Arberness. However, this time, he looks very different to how he did back then. Dare I say, it actually looks like he believes me now.

'I know that,' he tells me, affirming my wildest hope.

'You do?'

'Yes, that's why I'm here.'

'But how? I told you I was innocent before and you didn't believe me. Nobody believed me!'

'New evidence has come to light. It's evidence that I have taken to my colleagues.'

'Evidence? What evidence?'

I think of Greg then and how he promised me he was going to find a way of tricking Fern into making a mistake. 'He actually did it?'

'Greg recorded a conversation he had with Fern in which she told him several things that prove she lied to us,' Tomlin tells me. 'From what we've heard, Fern got revenge on you and Drew for your affair, and she used Rory to help her. Then she killed him when she couldn't trust him to keep it quiet.'

It's crazy. It's despicable. It's unbelievable. But it's the truth and, now I know it, I can finally make sense of this whole nightmare.

'She said all that? Greg recorded it?'

'Yes. He was very clever. And very brave.'

'I don't understand. How did Fern end up stabbing him? Did she find out?'

'I suspect so. I don't know exactly because the only two people in the hotel room where it all took place were Fern and Greg. He is dead while we haven't been able to speak to her yet.'

'Why not?'

'She hasn't been home since yesterday morning. I've had an officer watching her house who has orders to arrest her on sight if she returns. So far, she hasn't. Then I found out she was due to come here to see you.'

'Yes, that's right!' I cry, glad Fern isn't missing after all. It would be a cruel blow just as we have found out how guilty she really is.

'Okay, then we have to talk about what happens next. First, I want to apologise to you. We made a mistake. *I made a mistake.* Now it's time to correct it.'

I study Tomlin to try and get a read on exactly how he plans on correcting what is a lot more than just a mistake, but while I'm still unsure about that, I am warmed he has at least admitted to the fact he got it wrong.

'I'm free to go?' I ask, hopeful of being outside in the fresh air in a few minutes' time.

'It's not as simple as that.'

'Why? You just said you believe me.'

'I do, and you'll be pleased to hear that many of my colleagues in the force believe you too. The problem is, we can't begin the process of having your conviction quashed until we have Fern in custody and have questioned her over that recording.'

'Then arrest her when she comes here!' I suggest, wondering why it has to be so complicated.

'That is what I intend to do,' Tomlin tells me. 'Would you like to witness it?'

'What do you think?' I reply without skipping a beat, and Tomlin can't help but smile at my quick response.

'Okay, let's get moving then. Visiting time is due to begin in five minutes and I want everything in place for when it starts.'

I eagerly follow Tomlin out of my cell then, a spring in my step that has been missing for a long time. We join the warden who leads us past all the other cells on our way to the visiting room. As I go, I pass the cell belonging to Siobhan and, when I see her face peering through the slot, I pause for a moment to tell her the good news.

'That's wonderful,' she says, genuinely happy for me and for the chance I will be getting out of here soon, although I'm sure she must be a little sad, too, because it means she will be losing one of her friends in here. But I promise her that whatever happens, I will stay in touch, before Tomlin tells me we have to keep moving. One of the other cells I pass on the way belongs to Kelly, the bully, and when she sees me moving past, she sneers at me. I make sure to tell her what I think of her and make a few gestures in her direction to make my point even more clear, gestures that incite anger inside her, and she revels in telling me that I am 'dead meat' when she sees me again.

Hopefully, she'll never get that chance, though I am worried I might have been slightly premature as I follow Tomlin down a long corridor before we reach our destination.

'Please don't screw this up,' I tell the detective after I have taken my seat at the table. 'Arrest her and make sure she doesn't wriggle out of it.'

'I will,' Tomlin says before telling me that his officers are going to stay hidden out of sight to allow Fern to pull into the car park outside and make her way in, so that she doesn't get spooked and make a run for it before they can catch her. Once she is in the prison, she will be led in here as if everything is normal and, just as she sees me, Tomlin will swoop in and put her in handcuffs, giving me the pleasure of watching her arrest just like she watched me be arrested in her house in Arberness.

'Sounds good to me,' I say and I sit back in my seat and cross my arms, eager to get this show underway.

Looking up at the clock on the wall, I see that visiting hours have begun. Tomlin takes his place beside the door that Fern will walk through any second now. He looks just as excited as I feel. I know things are only going to get even more exciting when that awful woman is here.

Poor Greg. I can't believe she killed him. It sounds like he lost his life trying to save mine and, for that, I'll forever be thankful to him. My heart breaks for him, but I can't dwell on that at this precise moment, because things are still very much in play and Fern has not quite been caught yet.

Now where is she?

Five minutes go by. Then ten. It quickly becomes apparent that she is late.

Is she still coming?

Tomlin seems to be staying calm as he listens to his radio occasionally, so I tell myself to do the same, but when it gets to fifteen minutes, I am really starting to worry. It's after twenty minutes when Tomlin moves from his position by the door and comes over to see me. When he reaches me, he has some bad news.

'There's no sign of her outside,' he says looking as defeated as I feel.

'What does that mean?' I ask him. 'If she's not here then where is she?'

The detective has no answer for that one.

He just shrugs his shoulders and, as he does, I fear my freedom might be slipping away from me as quickly as I was almost released.

THIRTY

FERN

It's well past the time I was due to be at the prison to see Alice today. I skipped the appointment and, rather than spending that hour sitting across the table from the woman I framed for murder, I have spent it sitting in the car park of a motorway service station and trying my best not to panic. The problem is that it's not so easy. Having found out the police were searching my house yesterday, it's hard not to believe they have a reason to want to take me into custody, and with that scary thought constantly crossing my mind, it's hard not to go into full-blown panic mode.

As I stare through the windscreen of my car at all the people going in and out of the service station beside this busy motorway in the north of England, I am still trying to figure out what has gone so wrong for me in the last twenty-four hours or so. When I left Manchester yesterday to drive to Carlisle, I was not under any kind of a police investigation and was merely going to see Alice to get confirmation that Greg had been her one and only hope at screwing me over. Yet thanks to my nosey neighbour's text message last night, I know I dodged a bullet yesterday, because if I had been home when the police came then I'd be sitting in a cell and facing some difficult questions at present. Thankfully, I am still free, but I have to think carefully. If I had gone to the prison today to see Alice then I would have been arrested there. That's why I've not gone and, after checking out of the fancy hotel early this morning, I have been on the road ever since, reluctant to stay in any one place for too long because I have to assume I am a wanted woman.

But I still don't know why.

I see a little girl of no more than six or seven pass by the front of my car, holding onto her mummy's hand and skipping as they make their way back to their own vehicle. It seems silly, but I envy the little girl in that moment: she looks so happy and carefree and of course she should be because she is just a child. On the other hand, I am an adult with many problems and if I am on the run from the police, which I fear I might be, when is the next time I am going to honestly be able to say that I am carefree and happy?

Aware that envying and potentially resenting a little girl for being happy is not healthy, I look away from her and stare at my steering wheel instead.

Think Fern, think. Something has gone wrong somewhere. Some crucial piece of evidence must have come to light if the police searched my house. So what is it?

I'm not sure exactly how many minutes later it is when a horrifying thought crosses my mind. As soon as the possibility occurs to me, I really wish it hadn't. That's because if I thought I was anxious a few moments ago, I'm even more so now that I have considered this new possibility.

What if Greg sent that recording of my confession to somebody before I deleted it?

It's a horrifying theory but now I've stumbled across it, I am trying to think of anything I can to discount it. No, he can't have done. He didn't have time to. I dragged him into bed as soon as he left that bathroom. Then I picked up his phone, we had our fight, I killed him and then I deleted it. That's it. That's all that happened.

Isn't it?

It's no good trying to tell myself such a thing because the logical part of my brain offers up another scenario, and it is one that I cannot conclusively dispel. It's a scenario in which Greg had ample opportunity to send that recording to somebody while he was locked in the bathroom, and he only came back out once it had gone.

I have to face it – if Greg knew I was dangerous, and he obviously did after what I had told him, it would make sense for him to have a backup plan in case anything happened to him. While I'm sure his plan was to leave the hotel room when I was asleep and never be anywhere near me ever again, he must have realised there was a risk I would wake up and prevent him from doing so after I regretted what I'd said to him. Once he heard me knocking on the bathroom door, he would have known I was awake and, therefore, any chance of him making a sneaky escape in the dead of night was gone. He had to leave the bathroom and face me, and while he would have been planning on keeping up his act for just a little longer, he would also have known he was getting back into bed with a murderer.

So what would a wise man do in a situation like that?

He would send the piece of evidence to somebody else just in case they weren't able to do so at a later date.

I realise then I am gripping the steering wheel so tightly that my knuckles have gone white, and the palms of my hands are aching. So I let go before I reopen any wounds beneath my bandages. That solves one problem, but I've got absolutely no idea how to solve the bigger one. If Greg did send that recording to someone and it is now in the hands of the police, there is no way I can get out of this without going on trial for murder.

I could dispute what is in the recording and say that I was just drunk and talking nonsense. Would that work? I'm sure a good lawyer would have a go at making such a defence. The problem is, I said those words and now, instead of simply being seen as an innocent widow, there will be multiple people who think of me as a killer and they will never change their minds on that, no matter what arguments I put up to try and make them forget about it.

I thought I'd beaten Greg when I stopped him leaving that hotel room.

But what if he'd already won the second he left that bathroom and I just didn't know it?

I've been here too long. I need to get moving again. The police could be checking traffic cameras and I'm only thirty miles outside Carlisle, which is far too close to Detective Tomlin or anybody else who has a vested interest in my past. Just before I start my engine and get back on the motorway, I check my phone, picking it up from where it lies on the passenger seat beside me. When I do, I see that I have just received a message. It's not from my neighbour this time though. Instead, it is a private message on one of my social media profiles, and I recognise the name of the person who has sent it. It's from Miles Mayhew, the independent journalist of sorts who reports on all manner of things, including Alice's recent assault in prison and the man who went to visit her shortly before it.

The fact he has reached out to me at a time like this is troubling, and when I read his full message things only get worse.

Hello Fern. I'm Miles Mayhew of Mayhew News and I am contacting you regarding the case of your late husband, Drew. I hear the police have just come into possession of a new piece of evidence surrounding the case and was wondering if you would like to talk to me about it? You could give me your story. I'd make it worth your while.

There aren't many things in this world worse than slimy reporters sniffing out a story for clicks on a website, but hearing that the police have new evidence regarding a crime that you committed tops it. I must be right. The police must have that recording. Oh my God, what do I do now?

Trying not to panic, I type out a reply to Miles, doing my best to keep my response calm so as not to potentially add to any evidence against me in the future.

> *Hi Miles. I am not aware of any new evidence in my husband's case. What are you referring to?*

I hold my breath as I wait for Miles to read and then reply to my 'naïve' question, and it doesn't take long for the devious 'journalist' with the bit between his teeth to get back to me.

> *My sources tell me that it is an audio recording of you talking about what happened with Drew, Alice and Rory Richardson in Arberness. Do you have any comment to make on that?*

I throw my phone back down on the passenger seat as if it is suddenly on fire, and I don't even think about picking it up again or giving Miles any kind of a response. I've just got confirmation of what I feared.

Greg did get that recording out of that hotel room and now the police have it, they want to question me about it.

That means there is only one thing I can do.

The little girl who still looks so happy waves to me from her car window as I drive past her mum's vehicle. I keep my foot on the accelerator pedal as I leave the car park and get back on the motorway. Thanks to Miles and his 'sources', I don't plan on slowing down anytime soon as I head southeast, further away from Carlisle but also giving Manchester a wide berth too. That also means I'm staying away from Detective Tomlin, his colleagues and, of course, Alice, the woman who must know by now just exactly how she ended up being found guilty of a crime she didn't commit.

But just because she knows, it doesn't mean she can do anything about it.

Right?

THIRTY-ONE

ALICE

It's a very long walk from the visitors room back to my cell and it's made even harder by the fact I have to pass by Kelly's cell on the way. I was obviously very premature with my belief that Fern would be arrested this morning and I would be allowed out, as neither of those things have happened yet and, because of that, I am still stuck inside here. Now, according to Kelly, I am still very much in danger.

'I'm sorry. I promise you that I'm going to work as hard and as fast as I can to get you out of here,' Detective Tomlin tells me as we reach my cell, and the warden who accompanied us watches me walk back into my claustrophobic home. I've already requested my lawyer pay me a visit as soon as possible and, while that request was easily approved, my second one was not. I wanted to be moved to a separate part of the prison, a safe waiting area of sorts until all this was resolved and I could be released. Unfortunately, and as if they hadn't already done enough, it seems the police are not finished with making my life difficult yet because they told me I had to return to my cell for the time being, something I have very begrudgingly done.

'What happens if you can't find Fern?' I ask Tomlin as I re-enter my very humble abode, voicing my biggest fear before the detective has the chance to leave me here alone.

'We will find her.'

'But what if you don't?'

I'm aware that I sound like a needy child with my endless questions and desire to constantly seek reassurance, but I'm not sure what else I can do in my position.

'Right now, there is no way Fern will know that Greg sent us that recording before he died,' Tomlin tells me. 'As far as she is aware, she has got away again with what she has done.'

'Are you sure about that? If she doesn't know she is in trouble then why didn't she come here to meet me? It feels like she knew she'd be arrested, so she stayed away.'

'Again, she won't know we are looking for her here.'

'Won't she? Didn't you say you were at her house yesterday? What if she knows that?'

'She wasn't home, and we have had an officer watching her property ever since and she is yet to return.'

'So she hasn't been home for over a day and she is failing to keep appointments she has made. Doesn't that seem odd to you?'

If it does, which it should, Tomlin is not admitting it, and just repeats what he has already said to me about Fern not knowing the police are on to her. Unfortunately for him, I'm not buying it.

'Don't you see? She's always been one step ahead of us,' I say, hating how much that statement is true. 'So why are you so confident the same thing isn't happening again? For all we know, she has run away and every minute that goes by is a minute that she has a better chance of getting away with murder again.'

'We have officers looking for her everywhere.'

'Really? Where are you looking? Here? At her house? There's a whole country she could be hiding in!'

'Alice, please. It's important that you try and stay calm. You've done well to last this long and now we have this new evidence, this will all be over soon.'

'You don't get it, do you? She's tricked you once, and she's tricking you again.'

I throw my hands up in frustration and sit down on my bed while wishing my lawyer would hurry up and get here so I have somebody else I can speak to about this, as I don't seem to be getting anywhere with Tomlin. To be fair to him, he does look like he wishes he could give me better news, but he can't and that's the problem. There's nothing he can do that will help me unless it involves Fern being arrested and me being set free.

I feel nauseous again and clutch my stomach, wishing that this pain would leave me alone but feeling like it won't until this is over, which I fear it might never be.

'Are you okay?' Tomlin asks me and he takes a seat beside me. 'I can have somebody take a look at you.'

'I'm fine,' I mumble even though I feel anything but.

'Are you sure? You don't look it.'

'I'll be okay. Just get me out of here,' I urge the concerned detective.

'I understand how difficult this is for you,' says the man who gets to go home tonight while I'll still be stuck in here. 'Let me see what I can do about possibly having you moved somewhere safer.'

'Can't you just let me go? You already know that Fern did it, not me.'

'It's not as simple as that.'

'No, it never is, is it?'

I bury my head in my hands and feel like crying, but the sad fact is I'm too exhausted to shed any tears. I just want this to be over and, in some weird way, what has happened today is almost making me feel worse. It was one thing to face being found guilty of something I didn't do, but it's even harder to face having to stay in prison even though the police think they know I was set up. Damn how slow the legal system works. It's as if Fern is still laughing at me now, still getting revenge on me, still defeating me.

Will I ever be able to say I have got the upper hand on her?

'Please, just help me,' I beg, and that's the last thing I have to say before Tomlin tells me he will be in touch with me shortly. Until then, he is free to stride out of this cell while I am left to watch the warden lock the door behind him. As I stare at one of the many barriers between me and the outside world, I wonder how it can be that I'm in here while the real criminal is out there.

I lie down on my bed and wait for the nausea to pass and, as it slowly does, I try to think of something to make me feel better. I think of Arberness, my last home before this prison. The beach. The water. The friendly locals. A cold drink on a hot day at the village fete. The fresh air. The shops. The pub where there was always someone to have a chat with. Even after all that happened there, it would be good to be able to go back and see that place again. Hell, it would be good just to be able to see any place again that isn't this cell. But for now, I have to stay patient and trust the process that Detective Tomlin tells me is underway. While I do that, Fern is out there somewhere, free as a bird, spreading her wings and going wherever she wants to.

Where are you, Fern?

What are you doing?

Are you going to get away with it again?

THIRTY-TWO

FERN

I see the signs for Birmingham, but I keep on going, the dial on my dashboard sticking strictly to the speed limit on this motor-way. I'm making sure not to go too fast but I'm also making sure not to go too slow either, because not getting away quickly enough would be just as bad for me as getting caught by a speed camera.

I'm well south of Carlisle now, as I am of Manchester, but I'm still not far south enough to relax yet and, as I navigate the traffic as I pass Birmingham, England's second-largest city, I am fully focused on making it to England's biggest.

London is my destination, and it is amongst the sprawling capital that I plan to try and hide, hoping to lie low for long enough to figure out what I should do next. The police might think they got one step ahead of me by obtaining that recording of my confession, but I still feel I am one step ahead of them as long as they can't catch up with me. They won't know where I am, and while they will be looking, I've bought myself some time. I'll need every single second of it if I am to get out of this with my freedom intact.

As I forge on, my frantic mind is comforted somewhat by

the bank account I have with £5,000 in it. It's a bank account that I set up in my maidan name before I married Drew, and I still have access to it to this day, despite very rarely ever drawing money out of it before now. When I was younger, my mother always taught me to save for a rainy day, and that account was my best attempt at doing just that. I never told Drew or anyone else I had that money. What I expect will happen very soon is that the bank accounts in the name of Fern Devlin will be frozen, because once the police realise I have run, they will be desperate to stop me funding my escape any further than it's already got me. My hope is that they won't find the old bank account before I have had chance to withdraw more money from it. I've already taken £500 cash out from an ATM at a service station south of Manchester, and I plan to take out another £500 tomorrow once my daily withdrawal limit resets itself. Depending on whether the police find out about my old account will determine how long I can keep drawing on those funds, but I'm also aware that if they do find out about it, not only can they freeze the money but they will be able to see exactly where I was withdrawing it from and pinpoint my movements. That's just a risk I'll have to take, although I will make sure to never withdraw cash from anywhere that is too close to where I am actually staying for the night.

I suspect my best bet is to find myself a quiet bed-and-breakfast somewhere in central London where I can pay for my stay with cash and use a fake name. Whoever runs the establishment is hardly likely to suspect me of being on the run from the police, so I should be safe there for a while. Of course, I'll have to change my appearance. Dye my hair or buy a wig. Dress differently. Alter my accent. I'll also have to get rid of my car soon because the police will be looking for my licence plate. Maybe I can find a garage to sell it to. I'll most likely make a huge loss on it, but it could raise some more funds and I'm going to need as much as I can get.

I've been turning the radio on and off as I've been driving, because while part of me wants to know if my name is being mentioned on the news, another part would rather not know if that is the case. Is it better to be ignorant or in the know? I'm not entirely sure, which is why I keep hitting the button next to me and alternating between listening to the latest news bulletins and avoiding them entirely. So far, I have not heard anything to concern me. There's no report of the police hunting me, or any allegations mentioned about the things I might be guilty of. I hope it will stay that way, but I seriously doubt it, especially if a bloodhound like Miles Mayhew is already on the scent. It won't be long until a credible journalist finds out what is going on and, when that happens, my story won't just be flashed all across the website of *Mayhew News*. It will be on the front of the national newspapers and headlining the bulletins because, let's face it, it's not often there is a serial killer on the loose in England and it's even rarer that the killer is a woman.

The media are going to have a field day with this when they get hold of the story, and I can't help but feel them plastering my face all over their newspapers and websites is only going to make my job of lying low more difficult. It won't just be the police who are looking out for me then but members of the public too, and how is one woman supposed to stay hidden if there are millions of eyeballs out there trying to catch a glimpse? It seems like an impossible task but, then again, getting revenge on Drew and Alice seemed impossible and I managed that, so I have to have more belief in myself.

The main thing is that I find shelter, somewhere safe to stay, many miles away from where the police expect me to be, and once I'm there I can plan my next move. But it's thinking about my next move that causes me to hit my steering wheel in frustration and let out a cry of anguish.

I almost had it all. I had the house, the car, the dream life.

I'd won. I'd beaten those who had wronged me. *Then I went and threw it all away.*

It's unbearable to think that instead of residing in a huge house in a city I love surrounded by friends and familiar places, I am now going to be spending my time in a strange city in very humble accommodation with not a single ally to offer me support. I'm as alone as I have ever been, far more alone than people thought I was when I stood by Drew's coffin on the day of his funeral and dabbed at my 'tears' with a tissue. This is real. This is happening. I am officially a ghost, on the run and unable to ever tell the truth again. For a liar like me, that might not seem like such a big problem, but I know it's not that simple. It was Drew who made me a liar and, while I might have him to thank for me now being so good at it, I also have him to blame once again for the situation I find myself in.

I was happy being Fern Devlin, wife to Doctor Drew, living in Manchester and being content with what we had. I never asked for his affair or for us to move to Arberness, nor did I ask for all the ideas of revenge that came to me after that. I was just a scorned woman trying not to get hurt any more.

What am I now?

Who am I now?

I don't know the answers to those questions any more.

Or maybe I just don't want to admit them.

THIRTY-THREE

TOMLIN

As time goes by, it becomes more and more apparent that, somehow, Fern Devlin knew we were on to her and has fled before we can bring her in for questioning. I don't know how and can only hope it was just a slice of luck on her part, though it will be the last bit of luck she ever has. If I had to guess, I'd say she either saw the police at her house from a safe distance and ran then, or one of her neighbours called her and told her what was happening. Either way, she has not been home for a fortnight, and the more time that goes by, the less likely I feel it is that she is ever going to go back.

It's such a shame to see such a big house sitting empty but Fern has to know that returning to it will be a bad idea, so she has obviously fled, and I can't really say I blame her for that, not after what she said in that recording. If anything, her actions have almost done me a favour: she looks even more guilty. After all, innocent people do not run, do they? Her 'missing' status that began around the same time we tried to arrest her is more proof I need in my bid to get Alice's conviction overturned and all the charges directed at Fern instead. Thankfully, that is what is happening.

Along with the confession that Greg secretly recorded in that hotel room, a couple more things have come to light that prove to us that Fern has been lying. The first was when an officer interviewed the members of staff who worked on the hotel bar during Fern's fortieth party. While Fern told us that Greg was clearly drunk and that alcohol played a big part in how violent he would later be with her, all the bar staff that were spoken to reported that Greg had been ordering non-alcoholic drinks all night. They remembered it because he was the only person at the party who had been drinking them. That tells us Greg was not drunk like Fern said he was. It would make sense; while she thought he was just there to party like everyone else, we now know he was really there to do a job, and inducing that confession would have been harder for him if he really had been under the influence of several strong drinks. The fact Greg was completely sober at the time of his death was only backed up when the coroner's report was complete, further proving that Fern had lied about her partner being heavily intoxicated that night.

The other thing that has since caught Fern out is the footage from the elevator she took down to reception just after Greg had supposedly attacked her. While she made sure to look very much like the distressed victim when she was outside of that elevator, running around in desperate anguish, she was presented in a much calmer demeanour when she was alone in the elevator. Those few seconds it took to reach the ground floor were enough for us to see that, in the CCTV footage, Fern was perfectly calm and only became distressed again when the doors opened, and she ran out screaming to the receptionist.

It was clearly all an act, she obviously didn't count on there being cameras on her the whole time and she failed to keep that act up.

Alice should be released in due course and, whatever day she gets out of prison, it will not be a day too soon. I'll make sure to be there when she is released and will apologise again before wishing her good luck, though I appreciate it will be scant consolation to her. She's had her life ruined by Fern, just like my perfect record in correctly solving investigations has been ruined by her too, but bizarrely we are the lucky ones. That's because we're still alive to tell the tale of our brush with that dangerous woman while many others have not been so lucky.

I'm sure Drew, Rory and Greg would swap positions with us if they had the chance.

It's another grey day in Carlisle and I stare out at the gloomy sky as I wait for the kettle to boil. I'm in the kitchen at the police station, a kitchen I've stood in many times before and drank an ungodly amount of caffeine in during my time in the force. I'm searching for the positive effects of that legal drug again as I make myself a hot drink. I need all of the potency of the caffeine in my cup to power me through what is likely to be another frustrating and futile day.

The search for Fern is ongoing and has rapidly consumed my life and the life of my colleagues, both here in Carlisle and in Manchester. Detective Bell seeks Fern in connection with Greg's death, while I am seeking her in connection with everything that happened in Arberness but, so far, both of us have had to make do with what little information we have on where Fern could be.

My best guess is that she is in the south of England, potentially London, but she could be anywhere, I suppose. I know that she withdrew money twice, once in a service station near Manchester and the second time was the day after when she took out money in south London. The bank account she used was in her maiden name and her assets in there were frozen as soon as we discovered it, so while she did manage to withdraw a thousand pounds in total, there are thousands of pounds in there that she will not be able to ever spend unless she makes herself known to the police and is one day able to prove her innocence.

Another point we tracked her to was in Watford, the place she sold her car for £1,500 cash before boarding a train and departing it at London Euston; she then disappeared into the crowd, vanishing from the coverage of the CCTV cameras. That was two weeks ago, and that is where the trail ran cold. By now, I have to assume that Fern has changed her appearance, meaning it will be almost impossible to detect her on CCTV again. I also have no idea if she stayed in the capital or if she went elsewhere. She could literally be anywhere, but surely staying in a big city would give her the best chance of blending in. Then again, she might be lying low in a small village on the coast.

She fooled all the villagers in Arberness before, why couldn't she do it again elsewhere?

Taking my coffee and my weary body back to my desk, I slump into my chair and check my emails. There's plenty of things about small cases that are easily solvable, but there are no updates about the one large, looming case that continues to haunt me.

I'd give anything for a tip-off. A little nugget of information. Anything that might lead to us finding Fern. There have been a few calls from members of the public who say they think they might have seen her after recognising her from her photo in the papers, but none of them have amounted to anything yet. Many of those people have been mistaken and, even if some of them were right, by the time a police officer got to them and looked into it, if it had been Fern, she had always vanished, like a ghost.

What if she is dead? What if she couldn't bear to face the music and took her own life and now we'll never find her? That is a scary thought; I'm unlikely to sustain the motivation to help track her down if I keep thinking like this, so I dismiss the notion and take another sip of my coffee.

While I'm spending today sitting behind my desk, I have been out and about as much as I can to help with the search for Fern beyond the walls of this station. I've been in Manchester several times, assisting Detective Bell and her team as they conducted a more thorough search of Fern's property, though, sadly, no more evidence was found there, nor any clue as to Fern's whereabouts. I've also been to several places where Fern might have gone for help when she first realised she had to run, and that includes the homes of her parents and her best friends.

It wasn't pleasant to have to question Fern's mother and father about whether or not they knew where their daughter was, as they seemed like very decent people, and I knew what an impossible situation they were in. Either they did know where their daughter was, which meant they had a choice of either lying to the police or giving up the person they were supposed to be protecting, or they had no idea and were just as stunned as everybody else that Fern could do all those heinous things and then go on the run. Ultimately, I believed them both when they told me and Detective Bell that they hadn't heard from their daughter and that they wanted the same thing we did, which was for Fern to come forward and answer to the accusations against her. Unfortunately, none of us have got that yet. Us detectives have just got a prolonged headache while her poor parents have got to face the fact that the woman they helped raise was capable of some awful things, not least being able to run from her loved ones without saying so much as a goodbye.

I can't fathom how Fern's parents will cope if they never see their daughter again and don't get the closure they must so desperately want. I also can't fathom how anybody involved with that woman will feel if she fails to resurface. There aren't any winners in this, not even Fern: while she might be successfully avoiding handcuffs, I doubt she is having a good time in doing so, wherever she is.

Sometimes, when I go home at the end of a very long day and wearily take off my suit before falling into bed, I like to imagine that Fern is in a very unappealing situation. I might imagine her living in squalor in some grotty bedsit and hope that her stomach is rumbling and her throat is parched as she lies on a lumpy mattress and tries to get some sleep that never quite comes.

Other times, I'll imagine her sitting under a bridge, trying to stay dry as the rain hammers down around her and she contemplates how things could have been so different if only she hadn't been mugged and lost whatever money she had on her during the first few days on the run.

Of course, I have no way of knowing what situation Fern is in now: whether she is starving, skint and struggling, or possibly even doing well.

No one will know until we find her.

So, until that day comes, all I can do is hope that she is suffering just as much as everyone she left behind.

THIRTY-FOUR

FERN

There's a reason backpackers like to stay in hostels. They're busy places that are perfect for meeting people and making new friends. There's also a reason why people who aren't living the travelling lifestyle don't like to stay in them. They're noisy, crowded and almost impossible places to get some sleep. I might have enjoyed sharing a four-bed dorm room when I was eighteen and looking for adventure, but I can't say I am enjoying it now that I am forty and in desperate need of some peace and quiet.

My options are limited by my very delicate situation, so I am having to put up with sharing a bedroom with three other people, people who are total strangers to me as well people who absolutely cannot under any circumstances find out who I really am and what I have done before I got here.

The reason I'm in a hostel and sharing sleeping spaces now rather than having my own room in more private accommodation is because I am having to try and make my money last as long as I can, and staying here is much cheaper than going to a hotel. I've been officially on the run now for a fortnight, and my funds are dwindling rapidly, thanks in no small part to a couple of very unlucky incidents that left a big hole in my finances.

The first of those incidents occurred when I was staying in the first place I moved into when I got to London, which was a three-star bed-and-breakfast place in south London. I checked in under a fake name and paid for a week's stay with cash, and expected to at least have seven days there while I figured out my next move. However, things didn't go to plan. When I got back to my room one night after going out for a short walk under the cover of darkness, I discovered that somebody had been in my room and taken the envelope of cash I had hidden under my mattress. There had been £500 in that envelope, and I had been hoping that money was going to fund me through several weeks of cheap accommodation and basic food and drink, but it was gone. Angry and afraid, I went to the reception and told the owner of the B&B what had happened, hoping that he would help me and reunite me with my lost money. I told him that a cleaner must have taken it despite the fact that I had specifically said that I didn't want anybody going in my room at any time during my stay. Alarmingly, I did not get the response I had been hoping for: rather than being on my side and trying to help me, all the owner did was show me a smug grin and tell me that if I believed there had been a crime then I should call the police and let them come here to try and solve it.

It didn't take me long to realise that the owner had figured out that I was most likely hiding from something or someone, because a woman looking as nervous as me coming to a small hotel and paying in cash must look suspicious. He was calling my bluff, having guessed the police were not an entity I had any desire to talk to, and while he surely didn't know I was the killer woman mentioned in the newspapers, he was smart enough to figure out that there was little I could do to get my money back. I wouldn't be surprised if he stole that money himself, and it was probably my fault because he would have seen how much cash I had on me when I checked in, what with me so desperate to just get a room that I was dropping bank notes all over the place. Needless to say, I left that establishment as quickly as I could, but, being £500 worse off, my prospects were suddenly much worse than they had been before.

My bad luck only continued as I made my way across the river to the north of the city, and it was while I was eating a very cheap and rather sickly hamburger inside a fast-food 'restaurant' that I saw several police officers approaching the establishment. Panicking that I'd somehow been recognised despite having dyed my dark hair blonde and never going out in public without dark sunglasses on, I dropped my burger and walked away from the scene as quickly as I could, prepared to start running if I had to. It didn't come to that because as I glanced over my shoulder, I saw the police officers were simply going to get some food at the same place I had just been in, so I breathed a sigh of relief and figured the worst thing to come out of it all was that I'd left a half-eaten burger behind. Sadly, I was wrong; it was a few minutes later when I realised I had left my jacket on the back of my chair in the restaurant and it was a jacket with hundreds of pounds in one of the pockets.

I ran back to the restaurant but had to wait outside for the police to get their food and leave and by the time I went back in, the jacket was gone. Somebody had taken it and, while they probably thought they were getting a free item of clothing when they picked it up, they would have a lot more than that when they got home and checked the pockets.

That second slice of bad fortune meant I had lost almost half of my 'savings' in a matter of hours, and that was when fear started to set in. I felt as if I wasn't going to be able to stay hidden for much longer, what with my funds rapidly dwindling and no way of earning money for the foreseeable future. That was when I made the decision to find the cheapest accommodation I could, and I have been living in this messy hostel room ever since. But while my surroundings have been the same for the last few weeks, the faces have changed on a regular basis, and I have watched as several people have come and gone in this room.

There have been backpackers from all sorts of European countries who have stayed for a night or two while in London to see the sights and tick another place off their travel list. There have been a few locals who have just needed a cheap place to stay for a single night while they were in between whatever drama they were going through in their lives, all dramas that paled in significance to mine, I might add. And there have been people from different parts of the UK, including a couple of Scottish girls down in London for a hen party and some Geordies who spent the whole time moaning about how much more things cost down south compared to up north. Thankfully, there hasn't been anybody from Manchester because that would be a little too close to home for me, nor has there been anybody from Carlisle because that would have been very uncomfortable too. Needless to say, there hasn't been anybody staying here who originates from the tiny village of Arberness, although with my luck recently I wouldn't be surprised if that changed at some point.

The constant coming and going of new people in my shared room has been difficult for a number of reasons, not least because I'm always getting woken up in the early hours of the morning by people turning on the lights and packing up their bags. On the other hand, it has ensured that nobody has been around long enough to try and get to know me too well, and I'm grateful for that because this new life I find myself in is draining enough without having to tell lies every minute of the day. I'm confident that nobody recognises me with my new look and, if anybody does try and be friendly and ask me my name and where I am from, I have been telling them that I am called Grace and I am from the Midlands. That's usually an average enough answer to put a stop to any more prying questions, because let's face it, it's hardly as exciting as saying I'm Grigor from Romania or Alessa from Portugal, who are just two of the people I have shared this room with over the last few weeks.

The closest anybody has come to deeply trying to pry into my private life were the two Scottish girls, though that was mainly down to the fact that they were drinking lots before heading out for a wild night. They even tried to get me to come with them at one point, and while I would have loved nothing more than to have gone out and let loose on a dancefloor for a few hours and try to forget all about my troubles, I resisted and stayed behind, lying alone on my bed while the much younger women bid me goodnight and left, singing and laughing as they went.

There are lots of things that are unpleasant about being on the run and living under a false identity, but perhaps the worst is the loneliness. I've gone from being popular to having no friends at all, but if I want to increase the odds of staying out of custody, I know I need to keep it that way.

I'm currently in my usual position, which is horizontal on my bed and trying to read the free book I found on the bookshelf in the reception area downstairs. It's about the only entertainment I have considering I had to get rid of my mobile phone so the police couldn't try and track me and, occasionally, I am able to lose myself in the story on the pages. But it is only occasionally, and it is certainly not easy to read when there is so much noise being made around me by the three Italian backpackers I am sharing with tonight.

My room 'buddies' this evening are from Rome, and they tell me they are in London for sightseeing, but they've spent little time talking about Buckingham Palace and Big Ben since they got here and more time talking about where they think the best place to go to meet some English women is. One of them, a guy by the name of Vincenzo, even tried propositioning me earlier, offering to take me out for a drink, though it was clear from the way he was eyeing me up and down as he spoke that a drink was only ten per cent of what he had in mind for the pair of us to do.

I politely declined the plucky Italian's offer, and he hasn't spoken to me since, which only proves that he really was only after me for my body and not my conversation, but whatever disappointment he is feeling would surely be tempered if he knew what a lucky escape he just might have had. To him, I'm some boring, stuffy, older English woman who isn't up for a good time, but if he knew the truth, he'd pack his bags and get out of here as quickly as he could, probably running all the way back to Rome before telling everyone at home how he only just survived his brush with *the Black Widow*.

Yes, as I predicted, that is the unimaginative title the journalists in this country have labelled me with, ever since I went on the run and the news broke about what it was that the police were after me for. Whatever. I don't care what they say about me. All I care about is that nobody ever finds me and, so far, so good on that front. My evening takes an unwanted twist when I hear Vincenzo and his pals start talking about the news story that is currently gripping England, and as I listen to the three of them speaking my language in very heavy Italian accents, I realise they are talking about me.

'It's crazy. That woman is out there now and nobody knows where she is.'

'Imagine this happening back home.'

'Our police would find her quicker.'

'Maybe. Where do you think she is hiding?'

'Who knows? But they'll find her soon. She can't hide forever.'

I suddenly feel the need to get out of this room and away from this conversation, so I get off my bed and, ignoring Vincenzo's wandering eyes, I pull open the door and step out into the brightly lit hallway. Rushing into the communal bathroom, I go into one of the cubicles, lock the door and then spend the next two minutes being sick. Nausea is just one of the many symptoms I have been experiencing since I have been on the run, accompanying the symptoms of bad headaches and aching limbs, and as I flush the toilet and wipe my mouth with a piece of tissue paper, I don't ever remember feeling as bad as I do now.

Wiping away a few beads of sweat on my forehead and leaving the cubicle, I splash some cold water onto my face at the sink before looking in the mirror and staring at the reflection of the woman I have now become.

I don't feel like me, nor do I look like myself. My puffy and pale face is almost betraying me in the mirror, as if my outward appearance is unable to cover up the terrible secrets I am harbouring deep inside. I might be able to handle paranoid thoughts running through my brain but my skin clearly isn't taking all that stress quite as well and it's showing.

On the plus side, the fact I'm not looking exactly like I used to will only help me stay elusive. The less I look like the old me, the better, right?

But while I might be able to stay hidden, at what cost will it be?

I can't say I'm looking forward to finding out.

THIRTY-FIVE

ALICE

It's been two weeks since Detective Tomlin assured me that he was going to get me out of here, but in that time, the only thing that has happened is that I've been threatened again by Kelly and my mental and physical health has deteriorated to the point where I'm back in the prison hospital. I feel emotionally exhausted, sick all the time with anxiety and can barely sleep for the fear that Fern is never going to be found and pay for what she has done. It's little wonder that I require medical attention again, and, as a doctor takes a seat next to my bed, he has a sorry expression on his face. That doesn't bode well for him doing what I've begged him to do for me, which is prescribe me antidepressants, as well as any sleeping tablets he might be able to give me so that I might actually have a chance of getting some rest.

Sure enough, he doesn't have good news for me.

'I can prescribe you something to help you sleep, but it's mild,' the doc says. 'The best thing will be to address the issues for your increasing insomnia rather than simply try to medicate it.'

'My reasons for not sleeping? How about the fact I'm still

in prison for something I didn't do and the woman who put me here is walking free? If that's not enough, how about the fact that there is another prisoner on my wing who has already attacked me once and keeps threatening me with violence. Do you think those are good enough reasons not to be sleeping?'

I don't like to be sarcastic with somebody who is trying to help me, but it's either that or just get upset again, and I've spent enough time crying recently. Rather than dwell too much on what I have just said, the doctor moves on.

'As for antidepressants, I appreciate your difficult circumstances, and that is something we can offer. We will monitor you and offer you support and, for now, I am arranging for a regime of daily exercise for you that I believe will help your mood. Nothing too strenuous but you will be able to get outside and walk around more than other prisoners.'

'A walk in the fresh air? You think that's all I need to cheer myself up?' I cry, disgusted that this is the best I'm being offered. 'Don't you see? I'm not going to feel any better until I get out of this place!'

'I suppose we better do something about that then,' a voice says to my left and I turn to see Detective Tomlin has entered the room.

'What are you doing here?' I ask him, not exactly greeting him nicely, but I lost patience with pleasantries a long time ago.

'I have some news for you,' Tomlin says with a smile, but just before he can go on, my doctor interjects.

'There's something else I'd like to discuss with Alice, so if you could give me a couple of minutes,' the doctor says to Tomlin, but as I study the detective's demeanour, I can see that he is eager to tell me what he came here to say and that fills me with hope. That's why I ignore the doctor and demand that Tomlin come out with it.

The detective doesn't need asking twice and, as he steps

closer to the bed, the smile growing wider on his face as he does, he breaks it to me.

'Congratulations, Alice. I've just discussed this with your lawyer but he's kindly allowed me to give you the good news myself. The review into your conviction has finished and, based on the evidence against Fern, it has been decided that you are to be released immediately.'

It takes me a few seconds to process that spectacular sentence but, once I have, I start crying. However, for the first time in a long time, these are not tears of sadness but tears of joy, and as the detective becomes blurry, I don't even care about wiping my eyes to see him better again. All I can do is say thank you over and over again until saying it any more becomes silly.

'How about I give you guys a minute and then I'll come back and tell you how this is going to work,' Tomlin says.

I nod before the detective winks at me and walks back out of the room, leaving me alone again with the doctor.

Like the caring professional he is, the doctor hands me a tissue and gives me the chance to compose myself, which I appreciate because I am a blubbering mess.

'It's over,' I say, feeling exhausted but knowing that I definitely have enough energy to walk out of this place now that I'm allowed to.

'Congratulations,' the doctor says, though for some reason, when he says it, it doesn't quite carry the same sense of happiness as when the detective said the same word a moment ago. That's when I remember the doctor telling Tomlin that he had something he needed to discuss with me just before he was interrupted and, suddenly, I worry that the good news I've just received is about to be drowned out by some bad.

'What is it?' I ask, wondering what possible piece of bad luck is waiting for me no sooner than a little good fortune has come my way.

'I'd like you to take a pregnancy test,' the doctor says as a serious expression spreads across his face. But the only thing I do is stare at him for a couple of seconds before bursting out laughing.

'What?'

'I think you might be pregnant.'

'Pregnant? What are you talking about? I've been in prison! I'm not pregnant!'

'There were elevated levels of hCG in your blood test results,' the doctor tells me. 'It would also explain the sickness you have been experiencing.'

'The sickness? I'm sick because I'm stressed!'

'Then there is the fact that you look to have gained a little weight despite the fact you have told me you have hardly been eating recently. Your ankles are also slightly swollen and you have complained of headaches every time I have seen you.'

'The headaches are because of the stress too! And I've gained weight because I've been stuck in a cell for months!' I try, but the doctor seems to know more about this than me, and of course he does because he's the expert. But he has to be wrong. It's simply not possible.

'I haven't had sex for almost five months,' I say. 'So how the hell can I be pregnant?'

'Well, if you are, you conceived before you came in here.'

'Before I came in here? But that was ages ago. I would have noticed. I've had my periods.'

'According to the medical assessment that was undertaken when you were first sent to this prison, you said that you had always had irregular periods or very light ones.'

'What? Well, yes, but I've still had periods since I've been here?'

'Light ones.'

I nod.

'A little light bleeding during the first few months of pregnancy is not uncommon.'

'You've got to be kidding me?' I cry, my brain scrambling for an explanation as to why I am having this unexpected conversation only a few moments after being given news of my freedom.

'Look, I might be wrong, but I think you should take a test just to be sure. I can arrange one for you in here if you would like?'

I'm dumbfounded and can't even find the words to agree or disagree with the doctor any more. He seems to see that because he tells me he'll come back shortly, before leaving the room and giving me some time to gather my thoughts.

Pregnant? No, I can't be.

Can I?

The doctor seems to think so, but he must be wrong. I haven't had sex in ages. I haven't had sex since...

My mind goes back to that night in Drew's surgery, the night I first fell back into his arms after he had uprooted his life and followed me to Arberness. I'd told myself I wouldn't be charmed by him again, but I was and the affair restarted.

No, this can't be happening? I'm not pregnant and, even if by some miracle I am, the baby must be Rory's. It has to belong to my late husband. However, even though I think that, I already know it's nonsense, as Rory and I hadn't slept together for a while before his murder, which was just one of the many reasons I found it so hard to resist sleeping with Drew when he made his move on me again.

If I am pregnant, the baby is his.

I can't decide now whether to call the prison doctor back in here and give me the test or stay by myself for a little longer and try to keep existing in a state where I can pretend this isn't happening.

All I do know is that if I am pregnant with Drew's baby, this wouldn't just be a devastating shock for me.

It would be a devastating shock for Drew's widow too.

THIRTY-SIX

FERN

I hate going out in public because it's impossible not to keep looking over my shoulder and expect to see a police officer rushing towards me ready to say 'Gotcha!' But it has to be done, because I need to buy necessities, and as I enter the closest supermarket to the hostel, I am feeling as on edge as I always do when I come in here.

It's not relaxing to be around so many other people, nor is it pleasant to know that almost every aisle in this place is monitored by a CCTV camera. But needs must and I have to eat and drink, so I pick up a basket and get on with my shopping. However, in my situation, shopping is not as fun as it used to be, because I can't just buy whatever I want and pay little heed to the price tags. I'm on a strict budget and that means I can only really buy things I can afford rather than things I actually want. Instead of pricey chocolate bars and organic fruit and veg, I'm picking up cheap packets of noodles and bags of pasta that I can get four or five meals out of. It's amazing how many cans of tomato soup can keep a person under their budget. I'm going to turn into a bowl of soup or a plate of plain pasta if I carry on like this, but needs must and I hope it's not long until I can start buying slightly more appetising things.

Thankfully, my budget is due to get a boost soon by the wages that are going to start coming in from the new job I have managed to get for myself. As of next Tuesday, I will be spending twenty hours a week behind the counter of the local fish and chip shop, serving hungry customers their food soaked in salt and vinegar and receiving the very modest wage such work will earn me.

I'm not getting much money for that job, but I'll be paid in cash, and I didn't have to provide any form of ID to get hired there, so that's all I care about, and there is no doubting that the little money I will get from that part-time employment will ease a few of my worries about running out of funds anytime soon. It also helps that I'll have a free dinner every night because I'm told there's always leftovers, and while my waistline won't thank me for gorging myself on fish and chips every evening, my taste buds certainly will.

I make my way around the aisles of this supermarket, dropping cheap items of food into my basket as I go while doing my best not to look directly into any of the cameras that are fixed to the walls around me. It's stressful to be here, but it is nice to be out of the hostel for a little while, although it won't be long until I'm back in that crowded place and feeling lonely, surrounded by so many groups of friends who are all thriving while I'm merely surviving. Deciding that I need one indulgence on this shopping trip, otherwise I'm in danger of breaking down in tears at some point later today, I pick up a small packet of crisps and drop them into my basket, making a promise that I will treat myself to that snack while I am lying on my bed after my very unappetising dinner this evening.

It's not much but such a simple thing is enough to cheer me up ever so slightly, and I'm not feeling too bad as I make my way in the direction of the checkouts. But everything changes when I glance at the shelves that hold all the newspapers and magazines, because, when I do, I see a very familiar face staring back at me from the front pages of those newspapers.

It's Alice.

Desperate to know why she is in the news, I rush forward and pick up one of the papers, and I get a closer look at the headline that accompanies the photo of her.

Innocent Victim of the Black Widow Released from Prison

While it's galling to see yet another reference to my widow nickname mentioned in the news again, it's even more so to realise what has happened.

Alice is out of prison.

Reading the article that accompanies the photo of her, I learn that her conviction has been overturned based on the new evidence that came to light, evidence that confirms I framed her over Drew's death. The nightmare is over for her now and, as such, the revenge I took on her for sleeping with my husband is over too.

I can't exactly say she got away with it because she has still spent the last few months in prison, but she is now free to resume her life, while I am here, struggling so much with my existence. I wonder what she will do. Will she go back to Arberness? Will she return to Manchester? Or will she want to start again somewhere that has no connections to anything in her past? I don't know but her options are endless, unlike mine.

I grit my teeth as I finish reading the article before throwing the newspaper back on the shelf and hurrying to finish up the rest of my shopping. Alice is on my mind the whole time I stand queuing at the checkout, and she is still on my mind after I have packed my groceries into bags and started walking back to the hostel.

It's a nice day but I don't spend a single second more than I have to outdoors and just rush back into my dreary accommodation, walking through the reception area that is full of travellers with big bags on their backs waiting to check in before entering the kitchen and seeing a few people standing by the microwave. They ignore me and I ignore them as I put my bags down and begin unloading them, putting any items that require refrigeration into the bag that has my name on it. That's just one of many annoying things about living in a place like this. You have to write your name on everything otherwise people might take it, but even if you do, people might just take it anyway.

Hoping that I won't come back to the fridge later to find half of my food has already been eaten, I pack it all away before putting the rest of the things on a shelf, again with a label beside it with my name on it. That just leaves one thing I haven't put away and I carry that with me as I leave the kitchen and go into bathroom.

After locking myself in a cubicle and doing what I need to do, I leave it again and stand by the sink for a few minutes, staring at my reflection and wondering what is going to happen next.

By the time I look down at the pregnancy test in my hand, I get my answer.

It's positive.

I laugh then but it's more of a maniacal kind of laugh that reflects just how ridiculous my situation is. That awkward laughter is soon replaced by tears streaming down my cheeks, and I quickly become so consumed by crying that I fail to notice somebody else has just walked into the bathroom to join me.

'Are you okay?' comes the question from the concerned younger woman beside me, and I realise it is Manuela, a German backpacker with whom I had a brief conversation in the kitchen yesterday when she asked me if she could borrow a little bit of my pasta because she'd ran out of hers. I did her a favour and let her have a little of my food, and now it seems she is returning that kind gesture by checking that I'm okay.

'Not really,' I say, being perfectly honest, and when Manuela sees what I am holding in my hand, she starts to understand why.

'Oh,' is all she can offer before I drop the positive test in the sink and take a step away from it, as if doing so will help change the result it shows.

'This can't be happening,' I say before Manuela puts a comforting arm on my shoulder.

'Is the father around?' she asks me, probably thinking that things won't be so bad for me if I have another person with whom to share this impending responsibility. I just shake my head, which is the easiest way for me to let my new friend know that the dad isn't around without actually telling her why that is.

The dad isn't around because I killed him. I know that because this has to be Greg's baby. I came off birth control and we slept together just before I found out he had recorded me confessing to my crimes. It's his.

This baby belongs to the man I murdered.

'Do you have any family or friends who could help you?' Manuela asks me, but I just laugh at that question before crying again. If only this German woman knew why I couldn't possibly ask any family or friends for help then she would understand exactly why I am in such hysterics.

'What are you going to do?' Manuela asks me after I have stifled my sobs while staring at the test in the sink and wishing it would just disappear. It's funny because it was only a few weeks ago that I was fantasising about being pregnant and growing a child, and, now it's happened, it couldn't have come at a worse time.

'I don't know,' I say in response to Manuela's question,

finally looking away from the test and back to the mirror, where I see my tearstained cheeks and horrified expression staring back at me. 'I really don't know.'

For someone so used to lying, what I have just said is about as honest as I've ever been in my life.

EPILOGUE

ALICE

The water is as still as I remember it being and the air is as cool and fresh as always as I stand on the beach and stare at the Solway Firth, the picturesque part of the UK that separates England and Scotland. I'm officially a free woman now, out of prison, and my first port of call has been Arberness.

It feels strange to be back in this village, but I had to come here simply because it was the last place I lived before I was hauled away by the police and put through hell in the courts and in the prison system. This is where I lived with Rory, the man I cheated on with Drew, and both men died in this village, their lives ended before their time thanks to their association with Fern. It's a very grim chapter in the story of this little village and that's why I'm nervous about being back here. I'm not sure how the locals will react to me turning up again: while I might have just been proven innocent, many of them might still be unsympathetic due to the role I played in everything that ended up happening.

Some of the people here who I used to call friends may no longer wish to associate with me, possibly taking the view that my affair with Drew was what set Fern off on the warpath, and that means I have to take some blame for this sleepy section of the map now being notorious for all the wrong reasons. I guess time will tell on that front, and how things go will determine whether or not I end up staying here.

A part of me wants to as I still have some friends here for support and there is a sense of community that is sorely lacking in the cities, but I don't have to make a decision on it right away. There's a lot to think about and, for now, I'll just take one thing at a time, the first thing being actually processing the fact that I am currently carrying a child.

After getting over the shock of the prison doctor's suggestion, I took a test and, when I did, I discovered he was right. I am pregnant and because it took me so long to figure it out, I'm already halfway through that pregnancy. I thought all those changes with my body were the effects of the stress of prison life, but it turned out that many of them were due to the fact I have a little life growing inside me. That means it's not just me I have to think about any more. The wellbeing of the little life inside me comes first now and that will factor in to whether or not I decide to stay here in Arberness. This could be a great place for a youngster to grow up. The fresh air. The friendly locals. Attending a small school rather than an overcrowded one. Then again would it be cruel to raise my child in the place where her father was brutally murdered? How could I ever play with them on the same beach where her daddy met his untimely demise?

As I look around the beach, I see the lifeguard sign in the distance. It's a sign that tells anybody who visits this beach that, while there is a coastguard system in the area, anybody who enters the water is responsible for their own safety. But it's a sign that has a different meaning to me, as I know it as the place I agreed to meet Drew, not long after I found out he had moved here, to try and restart our affair. I met him on this beach under the cover of darkness and told him that he had to leave me alone, just like I had told him in Manchester, and as far as I knew, when I walked away from him that night, our affair was still a secret. Now I know that Fern was already on to us, there is every chance she had followed her husband that night and watched the pair of us meeting over there by that sign. That's a chilling thought, even more chilling than the wind whipping around me as I continue to stand here and contemplate a future in this place.

I left prison yesterday, my release made official, and my exit was accompanied by the apologetic Detective Tomlin who once again expressed his sorrow over what had happened to me before assuring me for the hundredth time that Fern would be found, and she would pay for what she did to me. Whether he actually believes that or not remains to be seen – she is still at large – but after telling me that, he then urged me to enjoy my freedom and not waste a single second of it on anything that didn't make me happy.

I fully intend to take his advice, although not quite in the way he perhaps imagines it.

I am going to spend my time doing things that make me happy now that I am out. First of all, I am going to take care of the life I am growing and, when the baby is born, I will strive to be the best mother I can be to my child. But there is something else I am going to do and it will make me happy, especially when I complete the task ahead of me.

I am going to find Fern.

I don't care what it takes and what has to happen along the way, but she cannot get away with this. If the police aren't capable of finding her then I will just have to do it for them.

Fern went to great lengths to get her revenge on me, so it's only right that I do the same in return. If she is keeping up with the news then I bet she had quite the shock when she read that I had been released from prison. However, that is nothing compared to the shock she will have when she finds out I am having her late husband's child.

She was the doctor's wife, but now I am the one who is having the doctor's baby.

I wonder what Fern will make of that?

I guess I'll find that out just as soon as I find her...

A LETTER FROM DANIEL

Dear reader,

I want to say a huge thank you for choosing to read *The Doctor's Widow*. If you did enjoy it and would like to keep up to date with all my latest Bookouture releases, please sign up at the following link. You can also download a free psychological thriller called *The Killer Wife* by joining my Bookouture mailing list. Your email address will never be shared and you can unsubscribe at any time.

www.bookouture.com/daniel-hurst

I hope you loved *The Doctor's Widow* and, if you did, I would be very grateful if you could take a moment to share your review. I'd love to hear what you think!

I also love hearing from my readers, and you can get in touch with me directly at my email address daniel@danielhurst-books.com. I reply to every message! Or you can check out my social media, where you can hear all about my adventures with my wife, Harriet, and daughter, Penny!

Thank you,

Daniel

KEEP IN TOUCH WITH DANIEL

www.danielhurstbooks.com

 facebook.com/danielhurstbooks
instagram.com/danielhurstbooks